Can you trust a ghost?

Sara stood alone in the dark playroom. *I can't believe this is happening,* she thought. *I'm friends with a girl who died before I was born— before my grandmother was born. And she's going to help me destroy the evil of this house!*

She hurried downstairs, aiming her flashlight at the floor. She couldn't wait to tell Michael what had happened.

Suddenly, the steps seemed to fall away from her feet. She looked down.

There was nothing there—she had stepped into midair. And she was falling.

Be sure not to miss
these other Trophy Chillers:

NIGHTWAVES:
SCARY TALES FOR AFTER DARK
by Collin McDonald

NIGHTMARE ISLAND
AND OTHER REAL-LIFE MYSTERIES
by Jim Razzi

THE RESTLESS DEAD:
MORE STRANGE REAL-LIFE MYSTERIES
by Jim Razzi

VAMPIRES:
A COLLECTION OF ORIGINAL STORIES
edited by Jane Yolen and Martin H. Greenberg

HOUSE OF HORRORS #1:
MY BROTHER THE GHOST
by Suzanne Weyn

HOUSE OF HORRORS #2:
REST IN PIECES
by Suzanne Weyn

HOUSE OF HORRORS #3:
JEEPERS CREEPERS
by Suzanne Weyn

HOUSE OF HORRORS #4:
AUNT WEIRD
by Lloyd Alan

Knock Knock... You're Dead

MEGAN STINE

HarperTrophy
A Division of HarperCollins Publishers

A Trophy Chiller is a registered trademark of
HarperCollins Publishers Inc., U.S. Reg. No. 1,814,912.

Knock Knock . . . You're Dead
Copyright © 1995 by Parachute Press, Inc.
All rights reserved. No part of this book may be reproduced in any man-
ner whatsoever without written permission except in the case of brief
quotations embodied in critical articles and reviews. Printed in the
United States of America. For information address HarperCollins
Children's Books, a division of HarperCollins Publishers, 10 East 53rd
Street, New York, NY 10022

1   2   3   4   5   6   7   8   9   10
❖
First Harper Trophy Edition

Knock Knock...
You're Dead

CHAPTER 1

"Help me . . ." whispered the voice. "Please help . . ."

Twelve-year-old Sara Buckner lay in her dark bedroom, staring at the ceiling. She had the strangest feeling that someone—or something—was up on the third floor.

"In the playroom," the voice called. "Please . . . come."

Sara shivered and pulled her yellow comforter tightly under her chin. She wasn't cold—she was afraid.

The rooms on the third floor were used only for storage. No one could be up there. It wasn't possible.

I can't go up there, she told herself. *Not in the middle of the night! Not to the playroom, and definitely not by myself.*

What was that? Sara's heart beat faster. She thought she had heard a bump coming from overhead. Like someone had knocked something over. Or bumped open a door.

She strained her ears, listening, but there wasn't any other sound. Just the strange feeling that wouldn't go away.

The voice called again. "I need you, Sara," it begged.

She glanced at the alarm clock beside her bed. The numbers glowed in the dark room. Two in the morning!

No, this is crazy! she told herself. She squeezed her eyes shut and tried to fall back asleep.

But how could she?

Sara had lived in Moonlight Mansion long enough to know that the house was haunted. Seriously haunted.

The 200-year-old house had been given to Sara's father as a gift from Grammy Rose. It had been in the family for generations, and Sara's parents were perfectly happy with it. But then, they never saw the things that Sara and Michael and their friends did. Like the monster that had attacked them in the graveyard on Halloween, or the weird purple eggs that hatched out deadly flesh-eating creepers. Or the baby-sitter who had seemed so nice at first . . . and tried to control Sara and Michael through look-alike dolls!

Only kids could see the evil that lived in Moonlight Mansion, or the *casa del mondo creepioso*, as Michael liked to call it—and in some ways that was the most horrifying thing of all.

I'm going back to sleep right now, Sara told herself firmly. She closed her eyes even tighter.

But she couldn't ignore the strange pull she felt. Her eyes flew open. Almost in a trance, she left her bed. She reached for the flashlight she kept on her nightstand. She had no idea who—or what—was on the third floor. But she was certain of one thing.

She had no choice but to go upstairs.

Okay, she told herself. *I'll just go up and look around. I can always call Michael if I need help.*

Sara tiptoed down the second-floor hall and peered up the stairs. The chill air from the third floor created a draft that seemed to penetrate her bones. She shivered and pulled her robe more tightly around her.

On the upstairs landing she paused and swept the beam of her flashlight back and forth across the long hall.

"In the playroom," the mysterious voice urged. "Hurry!"

Sara gulped. She hated the playroom. It had a hidden door that led to a room full of awful secrets.

Her heart started to beat faster. For a moment she wanted to run. *Turn around*, part of her was screaming. *Get out of here!*

"Please!" The strange voice was almost a wail. "You must help me!"

3

Taking a deep breath, Sara made herself walk slowly, quietly, toward the one room she never wanted to enter again.

Please don't hurt me, Sara silently begged whoever—or whatever—was calling her.

She stepped into the playroom. Shafts of bright moonlight streamed through the tall, uncovered windows. Sara's throat tightened. The last time she'd been up there, the windows were covered with faded velvet drapes. Now someone had opened them. Sara forced herself not to wonder who.

The room looked harmless enough. With its high ceilings and the oversize rocking horse at one end, it had probably once been a cozy, cheerful place. But along the left wall there was a huge tapestry. The woven picture showed three terrified children surrounded by wild animals with glowing eyes and bared teeth. What kind of picture was that to hang in a playroom?

Behind the tapestry was what Sara and Michael called the secret room. Sara could picture the tiny, windowless space. It was big enough to hold only a small bed and a bureau. Sara knew the room had once belonged to a young girl. But to her, the dark, airless chamber felt like a coffin. Sara shivered and swung her flashlight away from the tapestry.

Where are you? she wanted to shout. *Who are you?*

4

Holding her breath, she took a few silent steps farther into the playroom, closer to the tapestry and the hidden door.

Come out, come out, wherever you are! She fought back a hysterical giggle and licked her lips nervously. Was anyone really there? Was this where the thumping sound had come from?

BOOM! The playroom door slammed shut.

"You've come at last," said a voice at Sara's back.

Sara whirled around. And screamed.

There in the moonlight, hovering near the ceiling, was the hazy form of a young girl.

CHAPTER 2

"I knew you'd come," the girl said. She smiled shyly. "I just knew you'd help me, Sara."

Sara stared, trying not to panic. It was a ghost—it had to be. The girl's pale skin glowed faintly, and the long, full skirt of what looked like a nightgown swirled around her ankles. She seemed very young, perhaps nine or ten years old. Her blond hair hung in a heavy braid down her back. Everything about her was pale, except her eyes. They were huge and dark and burned with a strange brightness.

A ghost, Sara whispered. She'd already had a run-in with a ghost in this house. That one had looked exactly like her brother. It had tried to trap Sara and Michael inside an antique wardrobe. Sara tightened her grip on the flashlight and narrowed her eyes. There was no way *this* ghost was going to trap her anywhere.

The ghost's eyes widened in dismay. "No, please, you mustn't be afraid of me," she begged.

"I'm on your side, Sara."

"Wait a minute," Sara said, trying to keep her voice steady. "How do you know my name?"

"I've been watching you. I've watched the children of this house for ever so long—years and years. And when I saw you, I knew you were the one." Her pale face glowed with hope. "The one who could help me at last."

Sara eyed her warily. The ghost really seemed sincere. But how could she trust a spirit in this house? "Help you do what?"

"Help me defeat the evil," the ghost said, her eyes growing serious. "The evil of this house."

Against her will, Sara felt an urge of excitement. Defeat the evil! She'd give anything to get rid of the horrors that haunted Moonlight Mansion. Maybe—maybe this *was* a good ghost after all.

"Who are you?" she asked.

"My name is Elizabeth Carter," the ghost replied. "I was once a child in this house too."

"Elizabeth Carter!" Sara stared. "You're the girl who died in the secret room."

The ghost nodded, biting her lip. "That's right," she whispered. "Long, long ago . . . I died here, and I've been trapped here ever since."

Sara's heart went out to the little ghost. To have been stuck in this awful house for decades and decades! It must be worse than *living* here!

"I'm so sorry," she murmured. "I . . . why can't you leave?"

Elizabeth shuddered, setting her lacy gown aswirl. "There is a bad spirit in this house. Very, very wicked. It hates children. It won't let me go." The sadness in her eyes was heartbreaking. Sara felt an impulse to hug her, to comfort the little girl. But how do you hug a ghost?

"It hates children . . ." Sara repeated. "Is that why so much awful stuff has happened to Michael and me? The creepers, and the grave-yard monster, and everything?"

Elizabeth nodded. "That's right. And that's why I knew you were the one to help me. You defeated the evil every time! I think you must be the bravest child ever to live in this house."

Sara flushed with pride. "Well, I had lots of help from my brother. He's pretty brave too, I guess." *But he wouldn't have come up here in the middle of the night,* she added silently. It felt nice to have someone recognize how hard she'd worked to fend off the evil. Michael had a tendency to take all the credit himself.

Elizabeth wrinkled her nose. "Boys," she said scornfully. "Boys are dirty and mean."

Sara laughed. "Michael's a brat sometimes, but I wouldn't say he's mean—or dirty. He's pretty good about taking showers." She paused. "Anyway, he'd probably be lots of help with whatever it is you want me to do."

8

Elizabeth tossed her head impatiently. "No, Sara. I'm telling you, boys always mess things up." She leaned forward, floating closer to Sara. "It's not Michael's help I want, Sara. It's yours! You see, I know a way to get rid of the evil. But you'll have to do exactly what I say. And that means no boys."

"What is the evil spirit anyway?" Sara asked. "Is it someone who lived here once too? And why does it hate kids? Why can't adults see any of the horrible things that happen here? My grammy Rose won't talk about growing up here, but I know she must have—"

"Sara, you have to listen to me!" Elizabeth interrupted. She stamped her foot in the air. "Ignore me, and the house will continue to torment you. Obey and your troubles will end!"

Sara stepped backward, startled by Elizabeth's tone. "Obey you? I . . ."

"Oh, Sara, I'm sorry," Elizabeth cried, looking abashed. "I didn't mean to be bossy. It's just that I've been waiting so long for this, and it's hard for me to talk to you."

She wavered in the air, growing paler, more transparent. Her voice dropped to a frail whisper. "I'm not very strong, you see. I don't have much time. And there's much to explain to you. . . ." She flickered, fading out for a second.

Sara nodded in sudden understanding. She felt that same ache of sympathy that came when she saw an animal who needed help or was suffering. Elizabeth needed help—lots of it. "Okay," she said. "Tell me what to do."

Elizabeth closed her eyes for a moment, as if gathering strength. When she opened them, her gaze was dark and serious. "In three days the moon will be full. You must complete three tasks, one each night, just as the clock strikes twelve. I won't lie to you—the tasks will be difficult. But I know you can do it. You're *special*, Sara."

Sara looked at the floor, pleased and embarrassed. "What are the tasks?" she asked.

"Each time you complete one, I'll tell you the next. The first task is to find a special poem. It's in a book of poetry in the library. You must find the poem and recite it tomorrow at midnight when the moon shines on the fireplace mantel. Do you know about the carvings there?"

"Yes," Sara said eagerly. "They're the phases of the moon, right?"

"That's right. My father planned that when he built this house." Elizabeth closed her eyes again and seemed to struggle for the strength to finish. "When the moon is full, it will shine on the carvings. But that's not for a few days. First, you have to find the book."

"That doesn't sound too hard," Sara said. "But how will I know which book is the right one?"

"It's handwritten—a book of handwritten

poems. You'll find it in a locked bookcase in the library."

"In the library?" Sara furrowed her brow. "Oh, you mean the den, right? But how do I get the bookcase open? No one can find the key."

Elizabeth giggled suddenly. "But you did find it, Sara," she said. Her eyes twinkled with mischief.

"What are you talking about?"

"You had the key—when you and your brother opened the wardrobe in his room."

Sara's mouth dropped open. "That key? Oh, no, not that one!" She shook her head in dismay. "I can't use that!"

"Why not?" A shadow crossed Elizabeth's face.

"Because it's evil," Sara explained. "When we used it to unlock the wardrobe, an evil ghost came out."

Elizabeth looked exasperated. "I know, Sara, I was watching you, remember? But it wasn't the key that was evil, it was the wardrobe. You used it to lock the ghost back inside, didn't you? So it was a good key then."

"Maybe," Sara said hesitantly. "But, listen, Elizabeth, we buried the key out in the woods near the graveyard. I think it should stay buried. Isn't there any other way to open the bookcase?"

Elizabeth's eyes filled with tears. "No! You

have to find the key! Please, Sara—it's the only way!"

"But . . ." Sara shuddered, remembering the other ghost. It had spoken to Sara when Michael was trapped inside the wardrobe. *You're next*, it had threatened. *You're next.*

What if something evil came out of the bookcase when she unlocked it? What if an evil spirit tried to trap her inside?

"Elizabeth, I don't know about this," she began.

"Oh, *please!*" the ghost begged, her voice shrill with desperation. "Sara, you're my only hope!"

I don't have a choice, Sara thought. *I have to help her. How can I let her go on suffering— when there's a chance I could help her end the evil forever?*

"All right," she whispered. "I'll dig up the key."

"Oh, thank you!" Elizabeth cried, stretching out her hands to Sara. Sara shivered at her touch—it was the faintest pressure, a feeling like nothing Sara had ever known before. She forced herself not to pull away. Elizabeth was beaming, her eyes bright with joy. *I bet I'm the first friend she's had in a hundred years*, Sara thought.

"Find it, Sara. Find the poem by midnight tomorrow. I know you can do it—and soon we'll both be free!" With a faint final squeeze of Sara's hand, she was gone.

For a moment Sara stood alone in the dark playroom. *I can't believe this is happening*, she thought. *I'm friends with a girl who died before I was born—before my grandmother was born. And she's going to help me destroy the evil of this house!*

She hurried downstairs, aiming her flashlight at the floor. She couldn't wait to tell Michael what had happened. After all, she hadn't promised Elizabeth she wouldn't talk to him. And no matter what the ghost thought about boys, she and Michael made a pretty good team.

Suddenly, the steps seemed to fall away from her feet. She looked down.

There was nothing there—she had stepped into midair. And she was falling.

CHAPTER 3

The flashlight flew from her hand. Wildly, Sara grabbed for the railing. *Has that disappeared too?* she wondered frantically, but her fingers found the wood and she caught her balance. She took a deep breath to steady herself. When she looked down again, the stairs were as solid as ever. Her flashlight lay on the step next to her feet.

The house was playing its tricks again.

I hate this house, I hate this house, she chanted silently. *But now I've found a way to defeat it!* she thought. *And I'm going to do it. I'm going to do what Elizabeth says—even dig up the key—I'll do anything it takes! I'll get rid of this evil forever!*

Sara picked up the flashlight and hurried toward her younger brother's room. The door was closed, so she knocked lightly. She didn't want to wake her parents, whose bedroom was just down the hall.

"Michael?" she called softly, pushing open his door.

Michael's body was just a lump on the bed. He had the blankets pulled up nearly over his head. Sara shook his shoulder. "Michael? Wake up. Something's happened!"

"Huh? What's wrong?" Michael asked, sitting up groggily.

"Scoot over." Sara sat down on the bed. "Listen," she said excitedly, "I just went up to the third floor."

"Are you nuts?" Michael said, rubbing his eyes. "By yourself? At night?"

"Just listen. You won't believe what I found."

"What?" He stared at her.

"A ghost."

"What?" Michael's face twisted in panic. "A ghost! Not the one that looks like me!"

"No, no. Calm down," Sara told him. "Be quiet, or you'll wake Mom and Dad. Listen, this was a totally different ghost. A *nice* ghost."

"A *nice* ghost?" Michael sputtered. "What's that? One that says 'excuse me' before it sucks out your brains?"

"No, I mean it," Sara insisted. "This was the ghost of Elizabeth Carter! Remember the girl who died in the secret room? She was just a little girl."

Michael stared at Sara as if she were crazy. "Oh, I see. Just a sweet little girl ghost—who only wants to scare you to death?"

Sara sighed impatiently. "Listen, Michael, she didn't want me to tell you this. So if you don't listen, I won't tell you anything more!"

"Okay, okay," Michael muttered. "But I don't like this one bit."

"You don't have to like it," Sara said. "But you have to believe me, Michael. Elizabeth is a good ghost. She's not going to hurt us. She wants to get rid of the evil in this house! And she wants me to help."

"You're crazy," Michael stated flatly. "Help a ghost? In *casa del mondo creepioso*?"

"I know it sounds weird," Sara began.

"No. It sounds totally, completely *insane*," Michael said.

"It isn't, Michael. I think it'll work. Really."

"Well then, start at the beginning," he ordered. "How come you went up to the third floor anyway?"

"I heard a thump or something—I don't know," Sara said. "Then I heard a voice saying 'In the playroom. Please come.' So I went. And there she was."

"What was she like? Was she scary or freaky or what?"

"She was kind of sad," Sara said thoughtfully. "And funny too. And a little spoiled, and scared—like a kid. Michael, she was just like a little kid. And she hates this house, just like we do."

16

Michael shook his head. "I don't know," he said. "She's still a ghost."

"I know," Sara said. "But she's trapped here, Michael. If we destroy the evil, her spirit will be free. And so will we! Just imagine—this could be a totally normal house. Don't you see why I want to help her?"

Michael still looked uncertain.

"Well, I'm doing it," Sara declared. "It's worth the risk. I mean, things couldn't get any worse around here anyway." She stood up. "The first thing we need is to find a book that's locked away downstairs. So, hurry and get up. Because"—she took a deep breath—"because we have to dig up the key to the wardrobe to get it."

CHAPTER 4

Sara buttoned her jacket up tight. It was freezing cold inside the toolshed.

"Where's that shovel?" She pushed aside a couple of rakes and they fell, making a loud clatter.

"Shhh!" Michael hissed at her. "Do you want to wake Mom and Dad?"

"Sorry," Sara whispered. She switched on her flashlight and swung it around the small, cramped shed. A shovel with a pointed blade was leaning, half-hidden, in the corner. "Perfect!" she said.

Michael grabbed Sara's arm. "Are you sure about this?" He swallowed hard. "Okay, forget I said that," he mumbled when he saw the expression on Sara's face. "How are we going to find the key?"

"We marked the spot, remember? With three stones, set in a triangle."

Michael shook his head. "But it's buried in the

woods—near the graveyard!" He shuddered. "I really don't want to go in there. I don't want to find another half-rotted foot, like that one Gruff dug up. Don't you remember?"

Sara paused. Of course she remembered. How could you forget a rotting body that somehow turned into a monster? How could she forget how it had chased Michael, its loose flesh hanging from its bones?

She shook her head to chase away the image. "Listen, Michael, if we help Elizabeth, we won't have to be afraid of monsters anymore. Never again! Think about that, okay? Monsters, ghosts—they'll all be gone. This is our big chance. We've got to do it."

Michael took a deep breath. "I guess you're right," he said. "But I don't like it," he muttered, following Sara across the yard into the woods.

There were bats beneath the branches of the tall trees. Sara could see them as they flew through the air overhead.

This is creepy. Totally creepy, Sara thought.

Suddenly, one of the bats swooped down, diving straight for Michael's head.

"Yahh!" Michael screamed.

"Cut it out, Michael!" Sara frowned at him. "Someone will hear us."

Michael gave her a dirty look.

"Bats are actually very helpful animals," Sara said. "They eat mosquitoes, don't they?"

Still, there was something about bats at night . . . in the dark . . . in the woods. Sara shivered. *Don't be such a wimp*, she told herself.

"Wait!" Michael yelled again. "Did you hear that?"

Sara turned around. "What's wrong now? Hear what?"

"Footsteps," Michael said. "At least I thought so." Sara gave him an impatient look, but she stood still and held her breath, listening.

There *was* a noise—like something rustling in the bushes. "Yeoow!" Michael yelled. He swung the flashlight wildly toward the sound. Suddenly, the bushes parted. A large, dark shape sprang at them.

"Gruff!"

Sara laughed out loud. The big golden retriever jumped up, licking her face all over. "There's my boy, there's my love pup," Sara crooned. She ruffled the big dog's fur. Gruff leaped down and sprang up again, bouncing his big paws off Sara's chest.

"Okay, okay, calm down, boy." Sara turned to Michael. "Some monster," she kidded. "See, Michael? I told you. There's nothing to be afraid of." She hoisted the shovel higher on her shoulder. "Now, come on. And next time don't shout like that. You scared me to death!"

"Sorry," Michael said. He looked pretty embarrassed.

"I mean it," Sara continued. "We're all alone out here. After all, who would go tromping around in a graveyard at night?"

"You would," Michael muttered.

Sara laughed. She remembered what Elizabeth had told her. *You must be the bravest child ever to have lived in this house.*

"Yes," Sara said proudly, "I would."

She aimed the flashlight off to the right. "There—up ahead. I think the key is buried near that clump of trees."

"That's right near the cemetery," Michael said softly. They were close enough to see gravestones.

"So?" Trying to act braver than she felt, Sara walked toward the stand of birch trees. "Michael—look!" Just ahead, a few stones gleamed in the light of the flashlight. Sara pointed at them in excitement. "There they are!"

Three small rocks lay at their feet, placed in a triangular shape.

Sara dug the shovel into the ground and began to scoop out piles of dirt.

CLANG!

The shovel hit something hard. "That's it!" Sara cried. She dropped to her knees and started digging with her hands.

"Listen," Michael said suddenly. "Did you hear something?"

"Don't start that again," Sara snapped. She was getting a little tired of Michael's jumpiness.

She dug her hands deeper into the dirt. Her fingers closed around something cold. And hard. Was it the key?

"Sara . . . ?" There was something different about Michael's voice this time. As if he had trouble getting her name out.

Sara glanced up and froze. There, towering over her, was the body of a tall, hulking monster.

CHAPTER 5

Sara screamed.

A strong arm reached toward her.

"Nooo!" Michael yelled. He lifted the shovel like a baseball bat and swung wildly.

"Watch out," a deep voice yelled. "You're going to hit me with that!"

Sara stared. It was a man. A big, tall, strong-looking man, but not a monster after all. Definitely a human.

In her palm Sara could feel the key grow hot. The metal began to scorch her palm. Cupping it gingerly, she slowly stood up.

The man took a step toward Michael. His long hair and beard hid his features.

"Drop the shovel," he told Michael. "What are you doing? You kids have no business here at night."

"Neither do you," Michael answered, but he dropped the shovel on the ground.

"Yeah. You're trespassing," Sara added, trying to keep her voice from shaking. "We're on our own property. These are our woods."

The key pressed into her palm, growing even hotter. Sara gritted her teeth. It felt as though it would burn right through her flesh, but she couldn't drop it. She didn't want the man to see it.

"Digging near the graveyard—that's why I was hired," he said. "You understand? Some kids have been digging things up around here. I'm supposed to keep you out. I don't care where your property is."

"Hired?" Michael said. "You were hired?"

"That's right. I'm the new caretaker. I'm keeping watch in this cemetery now." The man squinted at Sara. "You say this is *your* property. Do your parents know you're out here? Maybe I should go tell them."

"Uh, they're not home," Sara bluffed.

The caretaker raised his eyebrows. "I don't believe you, young lady, but we'll let that rest for a minute. What were you doing out here anyway? You'd better tell me the truth."

"I—I was looking for this." On an impulse, Sara thrust the burning-hot key at him.

The caretaker grabbed it. He screamed in pain and dropped the key. It glinted against the damp ground.

"You lousy kids!" He waved his hand in the air to cool it off. "Just get out!" he yelled. "Get

24

out of these woods and stay out, you hear?"

Sara scooped the key off the ground and ran as fast as she could. Michael grabbed the shovel and took off after Sara.

"That's right—get home before I give you both what you deserve!" the man yelled.

As soon as she reached the yard, Sara slowed down. Breathing hard, she opened her palm. The key gleamed up at her. It was completely cool now, almost cold.

She stared at it. It was really very lovely. Long, nearly as long as her palm. And delicate. The top was curled in a fancy spiral. You'd never guess it had once unlocked a terrible evil.

"There it is," Sara said thoughtfully. "Michael—it helped us. Do you realize that?" She turned to stare at her brother. "It burned the caretaker. That's how we got away."

Michael shook his head. "Are you sure? Maybe he would've let us go anyway."

"Maybe. Or maybe not. Somehow, Elizabeth changed the key from evil to good," Sara said. "Maybe she knew that if we used this key for something good, it would become good." She curled her fingers around the key again. It was soothing against her skin, heavy and cool.

"We're going to do it, Michael. We're going to get rid of the evil in the House of Horrors! Starting with finding that book. Let's go!" She hurried into the house and flung her jacket toward a kitchen chair on her way to the den.

In the dark, the den wasn't exactly a friendly-looking place. Sara pulled the heavy curtains open, but it didn't help much. The pale moonlight cast long shadows onto the floor. The shadows were creepier than the darkness had been. Sara knew they were only the shapes of tables and chairs, but they were twisted in weird ways, as if they were reaching out to grab her. She found herself weaving around them as she went to the wall lined with bookcases.

The moonlight didn't reach the bookcases. They stood shrouded in darkness, heavy and gloomy-looking. It was too dark to read the titles of the books behind the glass doors.

"This place is really spooky at night," Michael said, waiting in the doorway to the room. He glanced around as if he expected to meet his evil twin ghost any second.

"You'll be all right," Sara said.

The locked bookcase was in the middle of the wall. Sara pulled the wooden library ladder over to it and climbed to the top step. She took the key from her pocket and rubbed it gently for good luck.

This is it, she thought.

Holding her breath, she fit the spiral key into the keyhole.

"Does it fit?" Michael called. He sounded terrified.

Sara felt the lock move. "Yes!" she whispered. "Be careful, okay?"

Sara closed her eyes. *What if another ghost comes out?* she thought. *What if it's a trick?* The evil wardrobe ghost's words echoed in her mind. *You're next . . . You're next.*

Sara twisted the key. Then, slowly, she pulled the glass door open.

CHAPTER 6

Nothing happened.

No evil spirit came flying out. No monsters reached out to pull her into the bookcase.

"Michael!" Sara cried. "Elizabeth told the truth. She really is trying to help us!"

"Well, maybe she is," Michael said. He didn't sound too sure. "Anyway, now what do we do?" Sara noticed he wasn't moving any closer to the bookcases.

"You're not still scared of this key, are you?" She took it out of the bookcase and waved it at him. "There's no evil in it!" She laughed at him. It felt good to laugh, now that she felt safe again. There was no evil in the bookcase. Elizabeth hadn't lied.

"Cut it out," Michael complained. "Keep that thing away from me."

Sara shrugged and tucked the key into the pocket of her robe. She turned to the shelves of books in front of her.

"How will we ever find the right book?" She shook her head in dismay. "Michael, you start with the bottom shelf. Look for a book of poetry."

Sara tilted her head sideways and started reading the titles on the top rows. *These aren't right,* Sara thought.

There were dusty old novels, mysteries, and history books, but no book of poems. She moved down the ladder and checked the middle shelves. No luck.

"Nothing," Michael announced. He straightened up and arched his back. "No poems."

Sara frowned at him. Where could it be?

"I could check the other bookcases," Michael offered, feeling braver now.

Sara shook her head. "No. Elizabeth said the *locked* one."

"But we checked every single book here," Michael protested. "No poems."

"It has to be here," Sara insisted. "It has to!"

She climbed back up to the top of the ladder. She was determined to check again and again. As many times as she needed to find that book!

"What on earth are you doing?" said a voice from the doorway.

Sara was so startled that she nearly fell off the ladder. She whirled around.

"Mom!" she gasped.

Mrs. Buckner stood in the doorway, tying the

belt of her fuzzy white bathrobe.

"Uh, we're just trying to study," Michael said quickly. "For a test tomorrow. For school."

"*Both* of you have the same test?" Mrs. Buckner raised her eyebrows. "You're not even in the same grade." She covered a yawn with one hand.

Uh-oh, Sara thought. *Think quick, Michael.*

"Uh, yeah," Michael stammered. "Well, *I've* got the test, and Sara was, uh, helping me."

Mrs. Buckner eyed him suspiciously. "A test in what?"

"Uh . . ." Michael looked around desperately. "Old books?"

Mrs. Buckner shook her head. "I don't know what you're really doing, but I want you both back in bed. Now."

"But, Mom . . ." Sara started to protest.

"But nothing." Mrs. Buckner's voice rose. "It's almost three in the morning!"

Sara slipped the key out of the keyhole and hid it in her pocket. "But it's really important." She tried one more time.

It is important. Sara seemed to hear Elizabeth's young voice saying the words. *It is important. It's a way to end the evil forever!*

Sara looked at her mother. She could see her talking, but it was as if she couldn't really hear the words. Elizabeth's words—the words Sara was imagining—seemed more real than whatever her mother was saying.

"Sara?" Her mother was looking right at her. She looked really angry now. "Sara! Are you even listening to me?"

"Yes, Mom. Sure," Sara said.

"Then act like it." She was using her "I mean business" voice. "Whatever you're doing, it can wait until tomorrow."

Sara backed down from the ladder. "Okay, okay."

Don't worry, Elizabeth, she found herself thinking. *I have to stop now. But I'll find the book before tomorrow night. I promise!*

CHAPTER 7

"Mandy! Wait!" Sara ran down the hall of Lakeview Middle School. It was late the next afternoon, and Sara was bursting with her news.

In the hall, Sara's best friend, Mandy Harris, turned around.

"Where have you been?" Sara asked. "I've been looking for you all day. You won't believe what happened!"

"I was late this morning," Mandy said. "And I skipped lunch. I had a makeup test in history." She rolled her eyes.

"I've got only a second to talk," Sara told her. "I have to go home to find something important."

"Well, I have something important for you," Mandy said mysteriously. She broke into a huge smile. "A message . . . from Jake Stone!"

Sara stood still. Jake Stone! He was the one guy she really liked. Really wanted to hang around. And he had a part in *Little Shop of*

Horrors, the musical the school was putting on.

Sara and Mandy were in charge of hair and makeup for the play, and Jake was playing one of the guys who got eaten by a crazy plant. Which meant that Sara would get to fix his hair—and put makeup on him. Actually touch his hair and his face!

Mandy took Sara by the arm. "Come on. We're supposed to be at rehearsal. I'll tell you on the way."

"I can't," Sara cried. "I really have to get home." She hesitated. All day she hadn't stopped thinking about finding the book of poems. It had been pretty hard to get through school. How could she possibly get through a play rehearsal too?

She had only until midnight to find it. And she had no idea where else she could look. She was hoping Mandy might have some ideas.

Mandy knew all about the House of Horrors. She'd even been bitten by one of the flesh-eating creepers that had hatched in the secret room. More than once she'd tried to help Sara and Michael defeat the evil.

"Something really major happened last night," Sara began. She motioned for Mandy to come closer.

"More major than talking to Jake Stone? He looks really cute today," Mandy teased. "Come on!"

"Mandy, really—I don't have time for this rehearsal," Sara protested.

"Listen, Sara. Jake wants to talk to you. He was all nervous about wearing makeup, and I told him you would speak to him about it. This is the chance you've been waiting for! What's wrong with you, anyway?"

"Nothing." Sara shook her head. Sometimes it was impossible to get through to Mandy.

"Good. Besides," Mandy added, "remember what Mr. Demetrios said? He needs the crew there today. If you miss a technical rehearsal without an excuse, you'll be kicked off the play."

"But that's so dumb!" Sara said. "I mean, we're not even *in* the stupid play!"

Mandy shrugged. "He says he needs us there, and he's being really strict about it. You can't risk cutting. If you get kicked out, you'll lose your chance to hang around and flirt with you-know-who."

But if I don't go home right now, Sara thought, *I might not find the book in time.*

Mandy led Sara into the auditorium. Sara looked around, taking in the scene. About twenty other kids were already there, gathered together near the front. Some members of the stage crew were pulling scenery around onstage. The costume people had scattered old costumes on a few rows of seats and were discussing which ones they were going to use for the play.

34

The lighting crew were rehearsing their cues. The spotlights blinked on and off every few minutes. Mr. Demetrios was running around from group to group, giving everyone instructions.

Mandy nudged Sara. "There he is," she whispered.

Sara spotted Jake sitting near the stage, talking to his friend Mark Ringle. Mark was playing the crazy dentist, Sara remembered. Both boys had their feet up on the seats in front of them.

Sara could feel her heart start to race.

"Come on." Mandy led Sara to the row of seats right behind Jake.

"Mandy!" Sara spat out at her, tugging on her arm. "Not there!"

"Don't be silly," Mandy whispered back.

Sara sat down, feeling torn. She was embarrassed, but she was also glad to be near Jake. *He's so incredibly cute*, she thought. *Even the back of his head is special*. She stared at the long waves of hair that curled along his neck, and nearly sighed.

Mandy started digging through her huge tote bag. "Don't be too obvious," she whispered. "Wait for him to turn around and notice you. He will. I guarantee it."

"Mandy, I really should go home soon," Sara murmured.

"Just give him five minutes. Concentrate. Try to send him your thought waves or something,"

Mandy ordered. She pulled a plastic bag out of her tote and set it on the seat next to Sara.

"Here, I need to ask you something." Mandy fished two wigs out of the plastic and held them up. "They're my mom's. One is fake hair and the other one is real."

"Real hair? From someone's head?"

"Yeah." Mandy shuddered. "My mom says people used to sell their hair to wigmakers."

"Gross!" Sara said.

Mandy nodded. "That's what I need to ask you about. One of these is for the female lead—Audrey. I think the real one is prettier, but it's so creepy."

"Totally," Sara agreed. "So use the fake one."

Mandy sighed with relief. "I was hoping you'd say that. The idea of wearing a dead person's hair—yuck." She shivered.

Sara reached over and plopped the human-hair wig onto her own head. She made a hideous face. Mandy burst out laughing.

"Stop—you're too good at that!" she cried. "You should have tried out for a part in *Little Shop of Horrors*."

"No thanks. I live in a shop of horrors already," Sara joked.

Jake Stone turned around. "Yeah—old Moonlight Mansion," he said to Sara. "I hear it's still haunted."

Sara felt her cheeks burn. She hoped she

wasn't flushing bright red. Mandy squeezed Sara's arm.

"Haunted? Uh, yeah . . . haunted. Uh, that's what they say," Sara stammered.

What a dumb thing to say! She winced. *He must think I'm a total idiot!*

Mandy gave a shriek of laughter, as if Sara had just made the most hilarious joke she'd ever heard. Jake just grinned.

"Hey, listen, Buckner," Jake said. "Go easy with my makeup, okay? I don't want to look like some kind of clown or anything."

Sara tried to sound completely cool. "No problem."

"All the guys feel funny about wearing it, at first," Mandy said. "But the makeup looks great onstage."

Sara nodded. "Yeah. Remember last year's play? You couldn't even tell the boys were wearing lipstick."

"Lipstick! No way!" Mark Ringle turned around and made a face. "You can't tell me the crazy dentist would wear lipstick."

"A crazy dentist might," Jake said. "But why would I wear it? I play a dead man. Won't I look weird in lipstick?"

"Yeah," Mark agreed. "But at least you could hide in your coffin, so no one could see you." He cackled, trying to sound scary.

Jake snickered. "Hey, and you could hide in

your dentist's office. In the closet, or something."

"In my torture chamber," Mark joked. "My
secret torture chamber that comes out when I
start the dentist's drill."

"A secret torture chamber!" Jake hooted.
"That's a great idea! Think Demetrios would go
for that?"

Mandy looked from one boy to the other. She
was grinning like an idiot and poking Sara in the
ribs so hard it hurt.

"Say something," Mandy hissed under her
breath. "This is so cool! Say something to him,
Sara!"

Sara stared at Jake. A secret chamber. A
secret chamber was the perfect place to hide
something. Like a special book of poems!

"That's it!" she shouted, leaping to her feet.
"A secret chamber!"

Mandy and Jake and Mark were staring at
her in surprise. But she didn't care. Without a
backward glance, Sara ran out of the auditorium.

CHAPTER 8

Sara hurried up the drive to Moonlight Mansion. She raced through the kitchen door. "Anyone home?" she called.

No answer.

She dropped her backpack on a chair and hurried into the front hall.

"Michael?"

Again, no answer.

She ran upstairs to Michael's room. He wasn't there either. Sara hesitated. She reached into her jeans pocket and fingered the key to the bookcase.

She realized she was a little afraid to face the bookcase alone. *Where is Michael anyway?* she thought.

She heard a whimper and looked down. Gruff was lying at the foot of Michael's bed. He jumped up to greet Sara, licking her hand and wagging his tail.

Sara gave Gruff a quick hug and a scratch on

the head. "Hi, love pup. Hungry, boy? Guess I'd better feed you—and everyone else."

With Gruff at her heels, she hurried down the hall to her own bedroom. Not counting Gruff, who was really the family dog, Sara had five pets: two parrots, Gomez and Morticia, two goldfish, Happy and Lucky, and a hamster—M. C. Hamster.

"Hi, guys. Hi, M.C." Sara lifted the hamster out of his cage. She cuddled him and then let him sit on her shoulder while she set out food and water for the other animals.

Sara loved her pets more than anything in the world. Michael had made up the nickname Animal Girl for her because she was so crazy about animals. She had a special weakness for anything that was small or hurt in any way. Anything that was suffering. Or trapped. Or helpless.

Like Elizabeth, she thought. *Elizabeth is like that—trapped. And helpless.*

Gently, Sara put M.C. back into his cage. "Sorry. Gotta run," she told him. Gruff sniffed at his cage. "Okay, boy, you're next," she promised the dog. "See you other guys later."

After she filled Gruff's bowl, Sara took a deep breath and walked into the den. She stared at the locked bookcase, wishing Michael would come home.

Just do it, she scolded herself. *Stop acting like*

a scaredy cat. Nothing bad happened last night. Nothing came out of the bookcase. She took another deep breath. *Do it for Elizabeth,* she thought.

She pushed the stepladder back into place and climbed up. Just as she was about to put the key in the lock, a voice called from the hallway.

"What's up?"

"Michael!" Sara cried, turning around. "Where have you been?"

"My math teacher made me stay late to help her load some computer software," he answered.

Sara had to grin. Michael was good with computers—and his math teacher wasn't.

"Did you find the book yet?" Michael asked.

"No." Sara shook her head. "But I had a great idea. What if there's a secret compartment or something? What if the book is hidden *inside* the bookcase?"

Michael slowly nodded. "Could be."

"So give me a hand," Sara told him. "We'll have to take all the books off the shelves to find it."

"Wait, Sara. What if there isn't a secret compartment?" Michael asked. "We'll do all that work for nothing."

"We'll find it," Sara insisted. She began to pull books off the shelves and stack them on the floor. "Come on!"

Michael joined her. Before long, there were

piles of books on the floor, on the sofa, and on the chairs. As each shelf was emptied, Sara inspected the bookcase.

"Exactly what are we looking for anyway?" Michael asked.

"I don't know," Sara admitted. "I'm not sure how to find a secret compartment."

"Of course not. That's why they're secret." Michael gave her a scornful look. "Don't you know anything? There's always a trick to them. Like in all the Arthur Manheim movies."

Michael was an expert on Arthur Manheim, a famous horror-movie star who had made dozens of cheapo films in the fifties and sixties. Michael loved them all.

"In *Secrets of the Mummy's Tomb* he had to press a button hidden in a mummy case to uncover the real tomb," he told Sara. "And in *Terror Beneath the City* he had to pull a special lever. Then all the water drained out of the sewers and there was a hidden chamber under the city."

"Great, Michael," Sara said impatiently. "Only those were movies. And this den isn't a tomb or a sewer. So that doesn't help me much."

Sara pointed to the highest shelf. "Anyway, that's the last one." She climbed up and began pulling books down two at a time. "It's *got* to be up here," she muttered.

"Maybe the ghost told you wrong," Michael said.

Sara sighed loudly. "She didn't tell me wrong, Michael. But she did tell me to do this alone. I'm beginning to think she was right."

She pulled down the last few books. Then she ran her fingers carefully over every inch of the empty shelf.

"Wait a minute," Sara said, her voice rising in excitement. "What's this?"

She peered closer. In one corner of the shelf there was a small bare patch where the paint had chipped off. Showing beneath the paint was a tiny crack. With her fingernail Sara scratched at it and a few more flakes of paint fell off. The crack went all the way along the shelf!

"What're you doing?" Michael called up to her.

"There *is* something behind this shelf," she told him. "This crack—it was put here on purpose."

Michael craned his neck. "Seriously? Let me see!" he said. "Get off the ladder."

"No way. I found it!" Sara said triumphantly. The crack was too narrow for her fingers. She needed something thin and sharp to pry it open.

The key!

Sara slid the spiral-topped key from her pocket. She stared at it, shining in the palm of her hand. It had opened the bookcase—so why not a secret compartment too?

Holding her breath, she wedged the key into the crack.

"Not the key again!" Michael cried from below her.

"Stop worrying, Michael. You're being a pain."

Sara forced the key in even deeper and tried to slide it along the length of the shelf. "It's stuck," she muttered.

"I told you not to trust that key!" Michael called. "You were crazy to use it."

But suddenly the key slid free. The crack in the shelf widened. It spread about an inch, and in the gap in the middle Sara saw a keyhole.

Sara poked her finger into the opening. "There's another keyhole here, Michael. I knew it!"

She put the key into the slot. *Please, please let this be all right,* she silently chanted. *Please, don't let any evil come out!*

The key turned easily in the lock. There was a soft click, and then, without a sound, the back of the bookshelf slid aside.

Behind it was a small compartment. And in the compartment there was a slim, dusty book.

"Yes!" Sara whooped. She glanced down at Michael. "So I'm crazy, huh? Then what's this?" Her fingers closed over the book. In the same instant, the secret panel slid shut.

Sara cried out in pain. Her hand was trapped inside the compartment!

"Michael! Help!" She cried again, tugging

wildly at her hand. *Oh, no! Oh, no—I thought I was safe!*

Sara twisted her wrist, trying to pull her hand free. But the panel only closed tighter, cutting into her skin.

"What's that?" Michael asked nervously.

There was a strange rumbling sound. It grew louder and louder. "Sara! Watch out!" Michael screamed.

Sara glanced upward. In front of her, the bookcase began to shift. It swayed gently from side to side, pulling Sara's hand along.

"Michael . . ." she whispered. "What's happening?"

The rumbling stopped. In its place there was a deadly silence. Then, as Sara watched in horror, the bookcase began to fall forward.

CHAPTER 9

Michael threw his weight against the bookcase.

"Move, Sara!" he yelled. "Jump!"

"I can't!" Sara screamed back. She tugged, but her hand wouldn't budge. The sliding panel felt as if it were crushing her wrist bones, and she felt dizzy from the pain. The ladder she stood on began to slide outward. The bookcase rocked farther forward.

"Help!" Sara croaked. "Elizabeth! Please help me!"

Her father's voice answered her. "Sara? Michael—anyone home?" Mr. Buckner stepped into the den. His mouth dropped open in surprise and a puzzled look crossed his face.

"What are you two doing?"

Sara blinked. In front of her, the bookcase was still. Completely motionless. It was attached to the wall again, built right into it, as solid as ever. No one would ever believe that it had swayed and shifted. No one would believe it had been about to crush her.

"Sara . . . her hand . . ." Michael said weakly.

"My hand—" Sara ran her tongue over her lips to moisten them. "My hand is . . . fine." She stared at it. Her hand was not inside the secret compartment anymore. There was no secret compartment. No compartment, no keyhole, no crack across the bookcase. Just an empty shelf, on which her hand was resting safely. And in her hand was a slim, dusty book.

"Look at this room!" Mr. Buckner frowned, gazing at the stacks of books in the den. "I came home early to get some reading done before dinner. But how can I work in this mess?"

Sara looked at Michael. He pulled himself together. "Uh, sorry, Dad. We, um, we were looking for a book."

Sara held up the book. "This one," she said in a shaky voice.

Their father looked surprised. "Must be some book," he said. "Well, fine. But you'll still have to get this place cleaned up."

"I'll start," Michael said. He began to pile the books back onto the bookshelf.

"You too, Sara," Mr. Buckner said.

"Sure, Dad." Sara's legs wobbled as she climbed down the ladder.

"Wait a minute." Mr. Buckner stepped up to the glass door of the bookcase, examining it closely. "Wasn't this the one that was locked?

How did you get it open?"

Sara gulped. "Uh, it just opened."

"Yeah," Michael agreed. "I guess it just needed one really good tug."

Mr. Buckner gave them a questioning look. "Huh," he said. "Well. Anyway, I could use a cup of coffee." He left the room, shaking his head. "Kids . . ." he muttered to himself.

Sara breathed a sigh of relief. She looked at Michael.

"Phew," he said. "That was a close one! Good thing Dad came in and stopped the bookcase from falling on you. You would've been *totaled*."

"*Dad* stopped it?" Sara frowned at him. "What do you mean?"

"Sure, he did," Michael told her. "You know grown-ups can't see the evil stuff that happens in this house. So, Dad came in and the evil stopped. The bookcase had to stop falling."

Sara shook her head. "Dad had nothing to do with it."

"Then who stopped it?" Michael looked puzzled. "Who else made the bookcase go back into the wall?"

Sara hesitated. *Elizabeth, of course. Hadn't she?* Sara had begged her for help. And she'd come through.

But somehow, Sara knew she couldn't tell that to Michael. It sounded so . . . weird. Even to herself.

Anyway, they had the book. Now all they had to do was find the right poem—after they finished cleaning up the den!

"Finally!" Sara cried as she leaned against the door to her bedroom. "I can't believe how long it took to put those books back."

"Yeah, but now we're done," Michael said. "So, give me the book." He grabbed for it, but Sara lifted the thin book out of his reach.

"No way! I'm the one who was almost mashed to death." Sara hurried to her bed and opened the cover.

The book's pages were old and thick. The edges of each page had turned brown, but the centers had stayed light. Still, it was hard to read. The poems were written by hand in fancy, old-fashioned script.

I wonder who wrote these, Sara thought as she carefully turned the pages. There were a lot of poems, all in the same confusing handwriting. Sara wondered if a man or a woman had written them.

"Well? Which is the special one?" Michael asked impatiently.

Sara began to skim the pages. "I don't know. They're really hard to read. And, so far, they all seem pretty much the same to me."

"Let's see." Michael leaned over and snatched the book away.

"Michael!" Sara jumped up in alarm. "You'll tear it! Give it back!"

"Why should I?" Michael turned his back to her. "I get to see too."

"No, you don't. Elizabeth said I was the one who should help her—remember?" Sara held out her hand.

Michael read a few more pages, but then he handed it back. She took it carefully and brushed off the pages he had touched.

"Hey!" Michael looked hurt. "My hands are clean."

"Just making sure," Sara said. She bent over the poems again.

"I don't know," she murmured. "None of these sound *special* to me. I wish we had some kind of a clue. Anything to help . . ."

"Sara!" Mr. Buckner's voice called from downstairs. "Michael! Mom's home! Come down and help with dinner!"

Sara sighed. "Great. Now we'll never find it!"

"Hey, I'll go ahead. You stay here and read a few more," Michael suggested.

"No." Sara's shoulders sagged in disappointment. She didn't know what to do. It had never occurred to her that finding the poem would be difficult. "Maybe I need a break," she told Michael. "We can try again after dinner. After all, we have until midnight, right?"

Michael gave her an encouraging smile. "Right!" he said.

Sara pulled out a scrap of paper to use as a bookmark and slipped it between the pages. Then she carefully laid the book down on her desk. She started to leave the room.

"Wait a minute," she told Michael.

She went back to her desk and pulled out a couple of spiral notebooks. She piled them loosely over the book of poems, hiding it.

"Just in case," she said.

"Whatever," Michael said. He turned to go downstairs. Sara began to follow him, but a noise made her look back.

The top notebook had slipped aside. As she watched, another slid off the pile. The book of poems lay in full sight.

Over the desk, a window was opened slightly, letting in a gentle breeze. The cover of the book lifted as if the breeze had pushed it. One by one, the pages of the book began to flip over.

"That's weird," Sara murmured. As she went to the desk, the small brass turtle that she kept on the windowsill began to wobble, as if the breeze were pushing it too. It was pretty old and had turned green and grimy, but Sara loved it anyway. Now, as she watched, the turtle toppled over and fell onto the book of poems, pinning the pages open under its weight.

"Sara! Michael!" Their father's voice was louder this time. "Are you coming or not?"

Quickly, Sara put the turtle back where it belonged. Then she piled the notebooks on top of the book again and hurried down to dinner.

CHAPTER 10

Dinner was awful. Not the food—that was great—spaghetti and meatballs, Sara's favorite. It tasted delicious, and somehow that made her feel more hopeful again. What was awful was sitting still while the book of poems waited upstairs.

After all, I haven't failed yet, she told herself. *There's still plenty of time to find the poem.*

And then, if she *did* find it, maybe she could ask the ghost some questions and finally get some answers. Like, had Elizabeth been in the den? Had she been the one who saved Sara from the falling bookcase? How Elizabeth had lived— or existed anyway—with the evil all around her? How did she get strong enough to finally appear to Sara?

And maybe the most important question of all: Who caused the evil in the house? And why was it after only kids?

The more Sara thought about it, the more

eager she was to see Elizabeth again.

"Sara . . . ?"

Sara looked up. Her father was giving her a funny look.

"You're about a million miles away," he said. "Anything wrong?"

"Wrong? No. I . . . uh, just have some homework to do. Better get started! Dinner was great. Thanks!" Sara pushed back her chair and jumped up. She was free!

Taking the stairs two at a time, Sara raced to her room. She glanced at her desk and stopped short. A chill went down her spine. The book was uncovered again. The notebooks lay in a neat pile next to it. And the brass turtle was sitting on the open page.

Sara swallowed hard. She walked to her desk and stroked the turtle. It felt warm to the touch. She bent over the open book. In the dim light, the letters of the handwritten poem seemed to straighten and darken, growing easier to read. She gasped.

Michael came up behind her, and saw the turtle. "Gee, you got all bent out of shape when I just *touched* that book. I can't believe you left that dirty turtle thing on it."

Sara looked him full in the face. "I didn't," she said. "Michael—this is it. The poem. The turtle was marking the page for me."

Michael stared at her.

Sara bent close to the book. "Listen to this," she said.

> *"Moonlight, moonlight, shining bright*
> *Give me powers of the night*
> *Let me feel the serpent's bite*
> *Send me into death's delight."*

"Weird," Michael whispered.

"I know," Sara agreed. "But it's sort of— mysterious, don't you think?"

"Mysterious?"

"Yes," Sara said. "Or magical." She stared at the book. She thought the poem really *was* special. Beautiful, almost.

Thank you, Elizabeth, she said silently.

"It just seems creepy to me," Michael said. He read the poem again and shivered.

"Just hope it works, Michael," Sara told him. "Just hope it helps Elizabeth end the evil."

Sara took her time getting ready for bed that night—although she didn't intend to go to sleep. After washing and brushing her hair, she changed into an oversize T-shirt and a pair of slouchy socks. Then she slipped the book out from under her pillow and read through the poem again. And again and again.

". . . send me into death's delight." She shivered each time she read the words.

At eleven o'clock the light in her parents' bedroom finally went out. Sara was so impatient, she could hardly stand it. If only midnight would hurry up and come!

Then there was a knock at the door.

Sara jumped. "Who is it?" she asked sharply.

"It's me," Michael whispered back. He slipped into the room, holding a baseball bat.

"What's that for?" she asked.

"Just in case," Michael said. He lifted it into an attack position.

Sara laughed. "You can't kill evil spirits with a baseball bat," she said. "And besides"—she frowned—"you really can't come with me. Elizabeth said she didn't want boys around. And she might not show up if you're there."

"But aren't you scared to do it alone?" Michael asked.

"A little," Sara admitted. "The thing is, Michael, you didn't see Elizabeth. She really needs our help. And she can help us too. No more evil, Michael—remember that. Whatever happens, it's worth it."

Michael didn't look happy, but finally he nodded. "Okay. I'll wait here," he said. "But call me if anything goes wrong."

"I will," Sara promised. "Don't worry, I will."

Michael left the room and Sara read the poem for about the hundredth time.

At five minutes to midnight, Sara crept to her

doorway. Her parents were asleep. There was no sound at all. Michael had probably fallen asleep too.

Clutching the book of poems, Sara hurried down the front staircase and into the living room. Moonlight seeped through the windows. She glanced at the fireplace. The carvings of the moon were in shadow. She took a step toward them and gasped as a blast of cold air hit her.

She shivered. It had never felt so cold in the living room before. It was as cold as . . . as the third floor, she realized.

Her heart began to beat faster. Maybe Michael *should* have come along—

BONG!

Sara jumped.

But it was only the antique clock near the fireplace. It had begun to strike midnight.

Bong . . . bong . . . bong . . . bong . . .

Sara held her breath. She opened the book to the special poem and planted herself in front of the carvings on the fireplace.

Bong . . . bong . . . bong . . . The moonlight shifted. A bright shaft of white light crept up the side of the fireplace.

Bong . . . bong . . . bong . . . Behind her, the clock struck twelve. The moonlight crept over the hearth as if it were looking for something. Sara stared as it crawled toward the carving of the full moon, a circle cut deeply into the mantelpiece. Just below the circle, the moonlight stopped. The carving seemed to glow with a faint light of its own.

Sara's hands were suddenly shaking so much, she could hardly hold the book straight. Her stomach twisted into a knot. She swallowed and forced herself to read out loud:

> *"Moonlight, moonlight, shining bright*
> *Give me powers of the night*
> *Let me feel the serpent's bite . . ."*

She hesitated before reading the final line:

> *"Send me into death's delight."*

As soon as she had spoken the last word, a chill ran through her that made her shiver uncontrollably from head to toe.

Thump . . .

Something was coming.

CHAPTER 11

"Elizabeth!" Sara cried in relief.

The small ghost had appeared in front of the window. With the moonlight streaming in behind her, she looked less like a shadow and more like a real little girl.

"You did it!" Elizabeth beamed at Sara and clapped her hands in delight. "You found the poem!"

She floated forward. As she came near Sara, she stopped and folded her arms across her chest. "But you let *him* help you," she scolded. "I told you, boys mess things up. You almost got hurt by that bookcase."

"That was because Michael was with me?" Sara gasped. "Oh—I didn't know—I thought he could help."

"Well, next time, no boys," Elizabeth said. "Or it won't work. I mean it."

"Okay," Sara said.

"Good." Elizabeth smiled again. "But, oh,

59

Sara, I *knew* you could do it. You're so clever!"

Sara smiled back at the ghost. "But—what exactly did I do?" she asked. "I mean, I did the task, but what happened?"

Everything looked the same to her. The living room was the same, and the fireplace, and even the moonlight. She peered closer at Elizabeth. Maybe her face *did* look a bit more solid, stronger somehow. But that might have been the ghost's expression. Elizabeth looked totally excited now, like a little kid with a new toy.

"This is so wonderful!" Elizabeth cried. "Or, how would you say it? Awesome! I knew you wouldn't fail me," she added.

"Well, it wasn't too hard," Sara said, bragging a little. "Just sort of scary."

Elizabeth's brow furrowed with concern. "I'm sorry you were frightened," she said. "I wish I could help you more." She hunched her shoulders, fading out a little.

Sara paused. "But—you *did* help me, right? You stopped the bookcase from falling? And you moved the turtle onto the book, didn't you?"

Elizabeth faded away almost completely.

"Wait!" Sara cried in panic. "Don't go. I won't ask any more questions, I promise. Except for, well, what happens now?"

"Now I must tell you the second task," Elizabeth said. "I know you can do that too!" She paused, moving closer to Sara.

"You must go to the attic. There is a box there with a carved snake on the lid. Inside, there's a knife with an ivory handle. The handle is also carved like a snake. You must bring me the knife at midnight tomorrow."

"That doesn't sound too hard," Sara said.

Elizabeth bit her lip. "There is more to the task," she admitted. She started to grow hazy again.

"Go on, tell me," Sara encouraged her. "Don't be afraid, Elizabeth."

"Well . . ." Elizabeth rubbed her toe against the carpet, looking scared. Her form was so transparent now that Sara could see the pattern of the wallpaper right through her.

"When you bring me the knife," Elizabeth whispered, "it must be dripping—with the blood of an animal."

Sara stared in a shocked silence. *The blood of an animal? How can I do that?* she thought wildly.

A loud whisper broke the silence. "Sara! What happened?"

At the sound, Elizabeth disappeared completely. *Poof!* She was gone.

"Michael!" Sara whirled around. "What are you *doing* here?" Sara cried.

"Um—I guess I was worried about you."

"I guess you wanted to ruin everything!" Sara said angrily. "You knew she wouldn't stay if a boy were hanging around! I told you that! You really blew it!"

Michael was silent a moment. "Yeah, maybe. But we always helped each other before. We always tried to fight the bad stuff together. Why don't you want me around this time?"

"I told you," Sara said, completely exasperated. "It's not me! Elizabeth doesn't want you around. I wasn't even supposed to tell you about her!"

"Well, I don't see why not," Michael complained.

"What's more important?" Sara demanded. "Hurting your feelings—or getting rid of the evil?"

She walked over to the couch and sat with her knees huddled to her chest.

"Well, what about the second task?" Michael finally asked. "What do you have to do?"

Sara's anger drained away. "Oh, Michael, it's awful," she said. "I have to find this knife in the attic and bring it to her dripping with . . . with animal blood." She could hardly say the words. There was no way she could deliberately cut an animal.

Michael whispered softly. "She wants you to do that? Animal Girl?" He hesitated.

"Well, I guess the first thing is to find the knife."

Sara lowered her eyes. "Um—not now," she

said slowly. "I'm way too tired. And anyway, I'd rather go to the attic in the daytime."

"No kidding," Michael said. He shivered. "The attic is a pretty creepy place. Remember that Halloween mask?"

"The one that got stuck on your face and almost suffocated you?" Sara nodded.

"Yeah," Michael said softly. "And the dolls— the two dolls that looked like us."

"And made us do things we didn't want to do." Sara shivered. "I don't want to go near those dolls again either," she admitted.

"Yeah. You're right—let's go tomorrow after school," Michael said.

Sara turned her eyes away from Michael's. "Sure."

She left the living room and headed back upstairs. Michael followed her.

"Okay. I won't be late tomorrow," he told her.

"Sure," she said.

But upstairs, Sara waited as Michael went into his room and closed the door. Then she crept back into the hallway.

She was going to find the knife tonight. Find it the way Elizabeth wanted her to find it— alone.

CHAPTER 12

Sara's hands shook as she felt her way along the hall to the stairs. She crept slowly in the dark, aware of the damp chill that poured down from the third floor. The cold got even worse as she reached the door to the narrow attic stairs. She grabbed the brass doorknob.

Stuck.

Sara tugged harder. *Why does every door in this house always stick?* she thought, exasperated.

With both hands twisting the doorknob, she put one foot up on the door frame and leaned back. Suddenly the door came loose. Sara flew backward, hitting the floor hard. "Ow!" she cried.

She stared angrily at the door. Her head hurt. But the door was open.

She was inside the stairway now, between the third floor and the attic. She held her breath. It was dark in there. At least the third-floor hallway had big windows and some light always filtered through. But no light could reach these stairs, even when the attic door stood open, as it did then.

Sara paused, waiting for her eyes to adjust to the darkness. Finally, she saw the outline of the attic doorway ahead of her.

She took a deep breath. *I can do this! I really can!*

Only two more steps to the landing. Two more steps, and she'd find the knife Elizabeth needed and—

BANG!

The door to the stairs slammed shut below her.

Sara spun around in surprise.

BANG!

Above her, the door to the attic slammed shut.

Sara was trapped.

I'm not afraid, she told herself. *I'm not!*

She took a hesitant step upward, but missed her footing and stumbled. Her hands flew out to either side to steady her.

That's weird, she thought. *These walls weren't that close together, were they?*

"No!" she screamed suddenly. "No—stop!"

The walls of the narrow stairway were moving—pushing closer and closer together. Sara's heart pounded. She stood, frozen in fear, while the walls moved in on her. In another moment she'd be crushed!

CHAPTER 13

The walls squeezed against Sara's shoulders. She twisted sideways, trying to make herself fit into the tiny space of the stairs. She pushed with her hands, with her feet. Nothing helped. The walls were moving closer . . . closer . . . .

She tried to scream for help, but the words stuck in her throat. Only a thin, strangled noise came out.

The walls closed around her body like a vise. She wrenched her head to the side, scraping her forehead on the rough wood. She gasped in pain. The walls were squeezing the breath out of her, squeezing her head so hard, she thought her skull would collapse.

No! No—I can't let this happen! she thought frantically. *Elizabeth needs me!*

"I won't give up . . . I won't!" Suddenly, her voice came out loud and strong. "Elizabeth . . . I'm coming. I won't let this house stop me!" she yelled even louder.

Could it be . . . ?

The pressure on her head lessened. Were the walls moving back?

Sara took a shaky breath. Her ribs ached, but she felt as though she could breathe again.

Yes! Yes—they were sliding back now! Soon the stairway was as wide as it always had been.

Sara cried out in relief. She was free. She hadn't given up—and she had beaten the house!

But her entire body hurt. Gingerly, she touched her scraped forehead and took a couple of deep breaths. Her breathing was hard and raspy. As she pushed open the attic door, a cloud of dust swirled around her. "Ugh!" Sara choked on the stale air, waving it away from her face.

The attic was as big as the whole house, but the roof sloped down to the floor in many places, dividing the space into many tiny alcoves. There were only two small windows to light the whole room, and they were covered with layers of soot and dirt.

Sara switched on the overhead light. It flickered, then stayed on. But the dust swirled thickly around, making it almost as dark as if there were no light.

Sara tried not to shiver. It was cold, it was dark, it was hard to breathe—but she wouldn't give up now. She couldn't.

She pushed her way forward and stumbled. "Ow!" she cried, rubbing her ankle. She had tripped over a wooden crate. The attic was crammed full of crates. And trunks, and boxes, and old furniture, and the stuffed grizzly bear that Sara hated. The only thing she liked was the old costume trunk. It was stuffed with long dresses and fancy old-fashioned clothes. But she knew there was no snake-carved box inside it.

The knife could be anywhere, Sara thought. She hardly knew where to start.

She groped her way to a stack of cardboard cartons and pulled one open. Ugh—she had to stick her hands in there, in the dark? She held her breath. Paper! She sighed in relief. A bunch of old papers couldn't hurt her.

"Ouch!" Paper cut! She stuck her finger in her mouth and licked off the thin line of blood. The cut really stung, but she had to keep looking. There was no carved box hidden among the papers.

She inched toward an antique mahogany chest of drawers. The top drawer stuck, and she tugged it extra hard. It gave way suddenly, and she tumbled backward. The drawer crashed onto the floor. Sara fell into a box of old records. They crashed around her, knocking into a box of empty wooden thread spools. Then something slimy crawled over Sara's arm.

"Yuck!" Sara leaped up before she realized that the slimy thing was only an old creepy crawler toy. As Sara scrambled to her feet, she slipped on the spilled wooden spools and ended up on all fours. The dust kicked up worse than ever, getting into her eyes and her mouth.

She couldn't see, she was choking, her finger stung, and her sides ached. Could anything else go wrong? As if in answer, the dim overhead light started flickering again. Sara felt tears sting her eyelids.

"I won't cry!" she muttered. "I won't!"

Just then, a thin shaft of moonlight broke through the thick dust. Sara glanced up. The light came through the small window that looked out at the backyard.

The window, a voice seemed to say to her.

"Elizabeth?" Sara raised her head sharply. "Elizabeth? Are you in here?"

Sara felt the same strange pull she'd felt when the ghost had first called her. Slowly, she straightened up. Her breath was still coming in short, scratchy bursts. She walked toward the window. Then she saw it.

There, sitting on the window ledge, was a small wooden box.

Sara forgot her aches and pains. With a cry of delight, she rushed to the window and snatched up the box. She examined it carefully. It was long and narrow, about eight inches long and three inches wide. The top was covered with a fancy carving of a snake. The snake seemed to coil around itself. Its mouth was open, as if it were ready to strike. Two sharp wooden fangs glistened in the moonlight.

This is it, Sara thought. *The snake box.* She turned to carry it downstairs.

Then the snake on the lid started to move.

Sara screamed and dropped the box. It clattered onto the attic floor. But somehow the snake had slithered off the box.

And it had grown. As Sara stared in horror, it sprang right at her.

CHAPTER 14

The snake aimed its razor-sharp fangs at her throat.

Sara screamed and stumbled backward, tripping over some old golf clubs. She ducked. The serpent struck—at thin air. Sara's fingers curled around one of the cold metal clubs.

The serpent coiled upright, getting ready to strike again. This time it aimed low, darting with lightning speed. Sara scooted back as the sharp fangs swiped at her leg.

Sara glanced down. A small bite mark showed on her leg, oozing a trickle of blood.

"Let me feel the serpent's bite," she murmured.

The snake reared back, ready to strike yet again. Sara lifted the golf club. She aimed and swung.

BAM!

She caught the snake on the side of its head. Instantly, it shrank in size.

"Yes!" Sara cheered.

She clubbed the snake again. And again. With every blow, the snake dwindled. It shrank to the size it had been on the box, curling and slithering across the floor.

BAM!

Sara blinked. Before her eyes, the snake was transformed back into a wooden carving. The carving oozed and bled as if it were melting wax. As Sara stared in amazement, the waxy carving puddled up and seeped into the box. It wasn't a carving anymore—it was a picture, a flat picture of a snake painted onto the lid of the box.

Open it, the voice seemed to tell her. Elizabeth's voice. Sara grabbed the box and yanked on the lid.

Inside, a sharp knife gleamed in the moonlight. Sara couldn't take her eyes off it. The handle was made of a hard, light-colored material, like bone. It was carved like the head of the snake that had attacked her. It glimmered and shone in the moonlight. Sara stared at it as if she were hypnotized. It was so beautiful. Dazzling. And it *didn't* come to life.

Sara peered around the living room. It looked so different in the bright moonlight. Everything looked softer, much nicer than it looked by daylight.

"This is a pretty room, isn't it?" Elizabeth

asked. "I always liked this room best."

Sara nodded, agreeing with her. It was nice to see Elizabeth looking so well. She didn't seem at all like a ghost now. Her cheeks were full and rosy. Her mouth smiled, with no trace of tension in her face. And her eyes—her eyes were the best. Her eyes sparkled and twinkled, like . . . like *moonlight*, Sara suddenly thought.

"I'm so proud of you," Elizabeth said. She clapped her hands as she did when she was especially delighted. "You are *so* special, Sara!"

Sara felt overwhelmed with pride. *I really am special*, she told herself. *I really can save this house!*

Suddenly, Elizabeth frowned in concern. "Did the snake bite you?" she asked.

Sara nodded.

"And you didn't say a word!" Elizabeth looked amazed.

"No." Sara cocked her head to one side. "I just felt—"

She stopped, trying to figure out what she really did feel. "I just felt proud," she said finally. "I did what you asked. I found the box and fought the snake. And now I've felt the serpent's bite—just like it says in the poem."

"Yes—'Let me feel the serpent's bite . . .'" Elizabeth recited.

". . . Send me into death's delight," Sara finished for her.

Elizabeth's eyes grew wide with horror. "No!" she gasped. "No—don't say that *now*. Not *now*!"

"Why? What's wrong?" Sara cried in dismay. "Elizabeth! What did I do?"

But before Elizabeth could answer, the bright ray of moonlight that shone through the window became even brighter. Stronger than Sara had ever seen it. The moonlight streamed past her shoulder. Sara turned. It moved up the sides of the fireplace across the room, and the whole fireplace seemed to glow. It looked like it was lit up, as if it had a light bulb inside.

Sara felt herself pulled toward it. She couldn't help it—she had to go closer . . . closer . . . .

The brilliant moonlight burned into the carving of the full moon. A wisp of smoke trailed out.

What . . . ? Sara thought. Then the smoke turned into a bright flame. It shot out of the carving. Sara leaped back in surprise. The flame grew bigger and brighter until there was a wall of flames shooting out from the fireplace.

"Elizabeth," Sara cried out. "Watch out!"

Sara turned. Elizabeth was standing across the room. Sara froze. She wanted to run to help the ghost, but she couldn't move.

Through the flames, she could see Elizabeth changing, her flesh melting away. She wasn't a little girl anymore—she was nothing but bones. She had turned into a skeleton.

"Elizabeth . . . !" Sara heard herself cry.

"What have I done? I failed you! I failed you!"

All around her, flames leaped higher. The couch burst into flame, then the chair and the rug. The entire living room began to smolder and burn.

Elizabeth—the skeleton—came toward Sara.

Sara could only stare. *Run*, her brain screamed, *run!* But she couldn't move. She felt as if her legs were planted in the floor.

She *had* to move. She tried to pull up one foot, then the other. Then, somehow, she was running, but it was like being in slow motion. The skeleton came after her. Sara pulled herself out of the living room and into the hall. The bright shaft of moonlight followed her. Sara reached for the front door.

Let me out, she silently screamed. *Outside— I'll be safe.* She pulled the door open with all her might. She was safe on the porch.

But the bony hands of the skeleton reached through the heavy door, piercing it as if the wood were no more than a cloud. Or a ghost. The bones latched on to Sara's wrists and pulled. The skeleton was dragging her back into the house, into the leaping flames!

CHAPTER 15

Sara woke with a start. She sat up in bed, her heart pounding. She looked around in confusion, and fumbled for her bedside light.

She was in her room. Next to her on the bed was the knife box. She remembered now. She remembered going up to the attic. She remembered fighting the house, then finding the wooden box and fighting off the horrible snake.

Then she had run downstairs to her room, so exhausted that she'd thrown herself across the bed. She must have fallen asleep. And had a nightmare about Elizabeth turning into a skeleton.

Sara's flesh crawled. *It's a warning!* she told herself. She shivered, recalling the dream. *It's a warning not to let Elizabeth down. If I do, I'll destroy her.*

Sara closed her eyes to shut out the picture.

It was only a dream, she told herself. *I won't let Elizabeth down.*

Now more than ever, she was determined not to fail Elizabeth. She would do whatever she had to do—anything to get rid of the evil and free Elizabeth's spirit. Anything.

She had to use the knife, had to bring it to Elizabeth at midnight. She would bring it as Elizabeth wanted, dripping with the blood of an animal.

Sara looked at the knife box lying on her bed. She got up and pulled her backpack off her desk chair. She shoved the knife box into the bottom of the bag, then brought it back and put it next to her pillow, just in case. She didn't want to take it with her, but she didn't know what else to do. She couldn't leave it home, where anyone might find it.

Gruff jumped up. Sara laughed and threw the stick again. Gruff chased across the lawn after it, caught it in his jaws, and hurried back to Sara.

"Good boy," she said. She drew her arm back and threw the stick even farther. She watched Gruff spring after it. He looked so happy. All he had to worry about was where a silly stick would land. He had nothing hanging over his head— like how to finish a task to save a ghost.

Sara gave an anxious glance at the sky. It was still afternoon. A nice bright, sunny afternoon. There was no trace of the moon yet, and there wouldn't be any for hours. Still, she was worried.

Midnight was coming closer.

Her backpack lay on the grass beside her. The knife was still hidden inside. Sara sighed. She had no idea what to do, how to complete the second task.

Gruff yelped. Sara blinked and knelt down to take the stick away from him again. He whined and waggled his entire back end. She knew that look. Gruff thought she was ignoring him.

The big golden dog crouched at her feet. Playfully, he started sniffing at her backpack and pawing it. He tried to push his nose inside the bag.

"Silly dog," Sara said.

But Gruff only got more and more excited. Sara watched him thoughtfully. *He's going after the knife box*, she realized. *What does he want with it?*

She reached down and unfastened the clasp. Gruff stuck his paws into the bag, working at it. The edge of the wooden box appeared. Gruff got more excited. He jumped back and barked a few times, then sprang at the box, then backed away again, whining. He looked up at Sara.

"Calm down, boy. It's okay," she said in a soothing tone of voice.

Sara gazed at the box. It looked completely harmless. Just a long, slim wooden box with an interesting painting on the lid. It didn't look dangerous at all. Kind of pretty, really.

She bent down and held it up, admiring it. The colors of the snake glimmered in the sun. She loved the way they looked, all shiny, like the inside of a seashell.

She hadn't looked at the knife since the night before. She opened the lid. The blade gleamed in the bright sunlight. Sara lifted the knife and held it up to the sun. The handle was almost transparent, she realized. She squinted at it with the sun streaming in from behind. It was pretty. Like moonlight.

Behind her, Gruff leaped at her, his big tongue hanging out and a goofy smile on his face.

Sara jumped up. "Cut it out, Gruff!" she said. The knife glistened and grew warm in her hand. *Like the key,* she thought.

Gruff came closer, sniffing at the knife. He whimpered in a strange way and cocked his head to one side as if he wanted to ask her a question.

"What a silly boy," Sara said. She laughed. "Such a silly pup. Are you afraid of this pretty knife?" She held it out to him. "See? It won't hurt you. See?"

A sudden thought came into Sara's mind.

She could cut Gruff.

No! She shook her head to chase the thought away. *No—I shouldn't even think about that!*

Gruff whimpered again.

It was the perfect answer. It would be simple to do.

Sara looked at Gruff. Her stomach felt all twisted inside. "It's a good knife," she told him. "It can help get rid of bad, bad things in our house. You'd like that, wouldn't you, love pup?"

What are you saying? she asked herself.

Gruff pushed his nose into her hand again. He trusted her. He wouldn't even fight if Sara reached out with the knife.

If Sara got rid of the evil, Gruff would be safe too. She could do it. Right here, right now . . .

Just a little cut, she found herself thinking. *Fast and clean. It wouldn't hurt him.*

"Sara!" A voice rang out behind her.

Sara jumped at the sound. She whirled around with the knife still in her hand. At the same moment, Gruff leaped up at her. The blade slashed through the air.

"Gruff . . . !" Sara screamed.

CHAPTER 16

"Gruff!" Sara dropped to her knees, letting the knife fall to the grass. The dog looked at her with his big, droopy eyes. "Gruff! Are you hurt? Did I cut you?" Sara grabbed him and looked at his face, then his paws. She combed her hands through his thick fur.

But there was no sign of blood. No cuts anywhere.

Thank goodness! Sara thought with relief.

"What's wrong with you?" Michael said, rounding the corner into the yard. "You're white as a ghost. Been hanging out with your friend Elizabeth again?"

"Not funny, Michael," Sara snapped. "If I don't figure out how to get animal blood on the knife by midnight, Elizabeth will be stuck being a ghost forever."

"Don't we have to have the knife first?" Michael asked, kneeling to tousle Gruff's fur. He let his book bag slide off his shoulder onto the grass.

Sara flushed, feeling suddenly guilty. She still hadn't told Michael about finding the knife on her own. "Um . . ." she faltered, "I already took care of that. See?" She picked up the knife from where it lay glimmering in the grass.

"No way!" Michael's voice quivered with indignation. "You went to the attic without me?"

He reached out a hand for the knife. Sara had to force herself to give in to him. For some reason, she was reluctant to let him touch it—but why shouldn't he?

"I . . . I couldn't sleep after all . . . so I went up last night," she fibbed. "I guess I was too keyed up after seeing Elizabeth again." She tossed her head, trying to act as if she hadn't done anything unusual. "Anyway, here it is. Now all we have to do is figure out how to get the blood on it."

Michael was scrutinizing the delicate blade. "Wow, this is some piece of work," he said. "Well, listen, Sara, I had a great idea. I was thinking we could watch tapes of all my Arthur Manheim movies. I bet they can help us. I bet Arthur Manheim had to do some weird task like this once."

Sara sighed. "Michael, I doubt we could use anything out of those movies."

"Why not?" Michael looked offended. "Those

movies are classics. I mean it—they're meaningful. Arthur Manheim faces every problem you could imagine."

Sara snorted. "Well, I can't imagine him dealing with *this* problem. Still . . ." Sara was almost glad Michael suggested it. Watching old movies might help take her mind off the task. "Let me feed the animals first."

"Sure," Michael said. "What should we watch? How about—"

Sara tuned him out as she checked that her pets had enough food and water in their cages. She stuck her hand into M.C.'s cage, and the hamster came over and nibbled her fingers. "You're a good boy, M.C.," Sara told him. *How could I hurt anything as sweet as you*? she asked herself. *Or any animal?*

"—so, at the last minute they switched the human sacrifice for a slab of barbecued spareribs," Michael was saying. He started laughing. "Pretty cool, huh? And then Arthur Manheim—"

"What? What did you say?" Sara turned around, startled. She stared at her brother.

Michael looked at her in surprise. "You mean you're really interested?" His eyes lit up. "I was talking about the scene in *How Not to Make a Human Sacrifice*, where the natives switch the human sacrifice for an order of fast food spareribs and—"

Sara jumped at Michael, shaking his arms. "That's it!" she cried. "Michael—you're a genius! Now I know how to do it! I know how to finish the second task!"

CHAPTER 17

At eleven forty-five Sara grabbed the knife box and a flashlight and tiptoed to Michael's room. He had gone to bed hours before, but Sara doubted he was asleep.

"Knock knock," Sara called softly, poking her head into Michael's room.

"Who's there?" Michael answered automatically.

"Boo."

"Boo who?"

"Aw, don't cry, little boy!" Sara didn't bother to laugh at her own joke. "Listen, Michael—I hate to do this, but I really need you to help me tonight."

Michael sat up in bed. "I thought Elizabeth said—"

Sara nodded impatiently. "I know. But I really need you. Someone has to stand watch. But you have to promise—don't come in the living room. Don't scare Elizabeth away again. Swear it!"

"Okay," Michael nodded. He peered into the hall. "Is Dad asleep already?"

"I'm not sure. That's why I need you. You'll have to watch out for him in case he comes down for a snack. Now, come on," she said, motioning toward the stairs. "And don't do anything except what I tell you to do."

Sara led the way, aiming her flashlight low. At the bottom of the stairs, she glanced out the high window over the front door. The moon shone faintly.

Sara led Michael into the kitchen. She took the knife out of its box. "Stand by the door," she told him. "If Dad—or Mom—wakes up and starts to come down here, get rid of them. Okay? Think you can handle that?"

Michael saluted. "Aye-aye, sarge," he barked.

"Not funny," Sara growled. "And be quiet." For a moment she was really sorry she'd asked him to help. But she didn't have much choice. If anything went wrong now, she'd blow the whole task. And she wasn't about to risk that.

Sara yanked open the refrigerator door and pushed aside a carton of eggs.

"There it is," Sara murmured. "Great." She pulled out a plastic-wrapped package. "Yuck."

Michael turned to look. "Yuck is right," he cried. "Liver?"

Sara crossed to the sink and slit open the plastic. Wrinkling her nose in distaste, she lifted the bloody slab of calf's liver.

"That's disgusting!"

Sara agreed with Michael. Little droplets of blood clung to the meat and dripped into the sink.

Sara raised the knife and brought it down in a wide arc. It sliced the liver into two pieces.

Splat!

One piece of liver fell into the sink, splattering blood onto Sara's arms. She felt sick. Grimacing, she held the other half and squeezed. A stream of blood splashed the blade.

"There!" she said triumphantly. "We did it. The knife is dripping with animal blood—and we didn't hurt anything."

"Yeah," Michael agreed. "As long as liver blood is okay. What if Elizabeth really wanted you to cut a live animal?"

"I couldn't do that," Sara said. "And it's too late to worry about that now. Here, turn on the water so I can get this blood off my hand." She shoved the liver down the garbage disposal and rinsed off her hand, holding the knife out of the way.

Thump!

"It's her!" Sara said wildly. She grabbed the knife box and tucked the bloody knife inside. Her heart started pounding so hard, it hurt. *Calm down*, she told herself. *Calm down.*

"Okay," she said, taking a deep breath. "This

is it. You wait here. And remember, if anyone comes, get rid of them. And *don't* come in the living room."

Sara hurried through the kitchen door and across the hall. She peered into the living room. No ghost. "Elizabeth?" Sara called softly. "Are you here?

There was no answer, so Sara stood in front of the fireplace and waited, holding the knife box. The clock ticked closer to midnight. Suddenly, moonlight spilled into the room. Sara glanced through the window. Outside, the clouds had moved across the sky. The moon was bright— and nearly full.

A moonbeam inched across the carpet. As it had done before, it crept up the sides of the fireplace, moving across the deep carvings. The clock began to chime. Bong ... bong ...

"Elizabeth?" Sara called again. Where was she?

What if Elizabeth was angry about the liver? Or what if she was mad that Michael was downstairs? What if she didn't come at all?

But as the clock struck twelve, Elizabeth appeared. Sara felt a wave of relief. "Elizabeth!" she cried.

Something about her was different tonight, although Sara couldn't figure out what it was at first. Her hair, her face, her antique white gown, were all the same. Sara looked down. The ghost wasn't floating off the ground. She was standing on the floor.

Elizabeth saw Sara watching and smiled. "You see? I have more weight now—just like you!" She hopped a few steps into the room, giggling with delight.

Sara held up the knife box. "I did it," she said.

"You did?" Elizabeth clapped her hands together in delight.

"Yes." Sara looked at the box in her hand. She felt a small burst of pride. She had completed the second task! She opened the lid and held the box out to Elizabeth. The knife handle gleamed in the moonlight. Elizabeth leaned over and peered at the knife.

"Ooh. Blood." Elizabeth made a face, wrinkling her nose at the sight. "I'd better take that," she said, lifting the knife from the box. She held it in the stream of moonlight. Sara felt an odd chill. The knife seemed to glow. The handle seemed pearly white, and the blade seemed to shimmer through the coating of blood.

Elizabeth lowered the knife. With a dainty gesture she dabbed her pinky into the blood. Then she licked her finger.

An annoyed look flickered across her face. "This isn't from a live animal!" Her voice was unusually harsh.

Sara giggled nervously. "What difference does it make?"

Elizabeth stared a moment, then gave a strained smile. "You're right. I'm sorry, Sara. You did a fine job. It *is* animal blood."

Sara felt enormous relief. "What about the house?" she asked. "Is the evil ever going away?"

Elizabeth nodded. "And soon the house will be rid of all bad spirits forever." She clasped her hands, and a joyous smile lit up her face. She looked radiant, happier than Sara had ever seen her. "And I—I will go to my grave at last, where I belong." She paused, looking at Sara with a wistful smile. Then, with a toss of her head, she said briskly, "But time is short. You must complete the third task tomorrow night—the night of the full moon."

She stooped and tucked the knife into its box. "Sara . . . this last task might be . . . difficult. Even for someone as brave and clever as you." She shrugged apologetically and looked at the floor. The color drained from her face and her whole body grew transparent again. Sara noticed that she floated away from the floor too, as if she were losing the strength she had gained.

"It's okay, Elizabeth," Sara interjected. "I can do it! I know I can!"

One more task, she thought. *One more and Elizabeth is free—and the house will be a regular, nice, safe place to live.* Never in her life had

90

Sara wanted anything so badly.

"I can do it," she repeated. "I'll find a way, no matter how hard it is."

Elizabeth stared at Sara, her eyes wide and troubled.

"All right, then," she said. "What you must do is bring me a lock of hair—the hair of a dead person."

Then she was gone.

CHAPTER 18

Sara looked both ways up the sidewalk, but the street was dark and empty. The downtown area was almost deserted at this time of night. There were only a couple of cars parked on the street, like the long, shiny station wagon nearby. But there were lights in a few of the buildings, including the building in front of her. That meant that someone was inside the funeral parlor.

Sara tried not to feel scared, but she couldn't help it. For about the hundredth time she wished she were at school, where she was supposed to be. There really was a dress rehearsal for *Little Shop of Horrors* that night, as she'd told her parents. Mr. Buckner had dropped her off at school at eight on his way back to his office. It had all worked out perfectly.

Her father would be out very late. There was some kind of emergency deadline at his job, and he had warned the kids he might have to sleep at the office. And Mom was working the night shift at the hospital, where she'd recently gotten a job. Michael was supposed to stay over at his best friend Max's house, and Sara was supposed to go home with Mandy after the rehearsal. But Sara had other plans for the evening. She had no intention of going to the dress rehearsal. Instead, she'd left the school and run downtown, to the funeral parlor. Now she almost wished she hadn't. She wasn't used to being out alone at night. She didn't like it.

Someone crossed the street up at the corner. Sara shrank back into the shadows. But it was only a couple of high-school kids, talking and laughing. They turned and went in the opposite direction. Sara breathed a sigh of relief, though nothing could make her feel calm. Not about this.

Behind her, the light from the street lamp threw its reflection onto the window of the funeral parlor. She couldn't see in at all. She couldn't even tell if there was a shade covering the window, or if anyone inside could see her standing outside.

She felt around the window ledge, hoping it was unlocked. But it was shut tight. She had to think of *something*.

She had run out of time. Tonight was the night of the full moon. Now, tonight, she had to cut a lock of hair from a dead person.

Elizabeth needs this, Sara had told herself

over and over. She felt sick at the very idea. Cut the hair from a dead body? It was unthinkable. But she had to do it for Elizabeth. For all of them—her family, her pets, everyone she loved. She had to get rid of the evil.

At first she'd thought of the cemetery. Could she dig up a dead body and cut its hair? But even if she had the nerve to do that—and she didn't think she did—there was the caretaker to think of. He was out there every night, probably waiting for her to show up again. There was no telling what he'd do to her this time. No, there was no way to dig up a body in the graveyard. Michael had definitely agreed with her on that one. Finally, she'd thought of the funeral parlor. She could sneak in, find a body, cut its hair, and sneak out again.

I can do it, Sara told herself. Elizabeth's praise rang in her head. *You're brave . . . you're so clever . . . so special . . . you can get rid of the evil . . . the evil. . . .*

It might not be so bad. Dead people were just like people sleeping, weren't they?

Sara moved around the building, looking for another way in. A strip of light caught her eye. Someone had left the back door open a crack. All she had to do was push her way inside.

Sara closed her eyes and willed herself to be calm. She wasn't a real criminal, after all. She could pretend that she was some kind of adventurer, like the hero in a movie who had to break into a building to help someone in need. That's all she was doing. She was just trying to help someone. She—

"Psst!" Someone grabbed her shoulder.

Sara screamed. So did the other person.

Sara whirled around. "Mandy! What are you doing here?"

Mandy looked at her in surprise. "My mom was driving me to rehearsal. We saw you here and thought you got lost or something. So I made her drop me off too. We can walk up to school together. It's only a couple blocks away."

Sara shook her head. "Look, Mandy, I can't go to rehearsal. I—oh, just go away and leave me alone!"

Mandy looked stung.

"Oh, Mandy," Sara cried, "you don't under-stand—"

"What is wrong with you anyway?" A hurt look came into Mandy's eyes. "You've been acting so weird lately. You blew off rehearsal again yesterday and didn't even tell me! Look, if you don't want to be friends anymore . . ."

"No!" Sara cried. "It isn't that. It's just . . ." She hesitated, and then it all came pouring out. She told Mandy all about the tasks: the poem, the knife—and then the last thing she was supposed to do. About cutting the hair from a dead person. How she couldn't face the cemetery.

Mandy stared at her in shock. "I can't believe you'd even consider it," she said.

"I had to think of something. I tried everything else," Sara told her. "I called all the hospitals in town, but they wouldn't let me inspect a dead body—not even for a 'science' project."

"I can't believe this," Mandy repeated.

"Believe it," Sara said grimly. "I called Lisa Tate—her older sister is in medical school. I thought maybe she could find a corpse. But her sister goes to medical school in Colorado! I even asked Shannon Smith's father if I could come into the police morgue for a tour. He said I needed a parent's permission first."

"This is incredible," Mandy murmured.

"I know," Sara agreed. "And this is the best idea I had. To sneak into the funeral home." She pointed at the open door. "The door is open and everything. All we have to do is slip inside and find a body." She paused. "Would you come with me?"

Mandy stared at her. "Me? Sneak into the funeral home?" Mandy stared at the closed window in front of them. "And go inside and cut off some dead person's hair?"

"It *is* only hair," Sara said. "It's not like I have to bring her the whole body."

Mandy shook her head. "No way!"

"I know it's awful!" Sara cried. "But, Mandy—you don't know how horrible my house is. You don't know what it's like to wake up every morning and wonder what might happen. And I can stop all that! I can end it for good!"

"Okay, okay," Mandy said, trying to calm Sara down. "I *do* understand. A little. I know your house is awful. Don't forget—I got bitten by one of those creeper things!"

"Then you *should* help me. Please," Sara begged. "I don't want to do it alone."

"What if someone catches us?" Mandy looked worried. "We'll be arrested! Who'll stop the evil if you end up in jail?"

"We can't think about that. This is too important." Sara grabbed Mandy's hand. "At least do what Michael did. Just stand watch, okay?"

"I don't have to go inside?"

"No," Sara promised.

Mandy hesitated. "Well, I must be crazy—but, okay," she said.

Sara threw her arms around her and hugged her tight. "Thank you! You're the very best friend in the whole wide world!"

"Or the stupidest," Mandy muttered. She positioned herself a few feet from the back door, where she could watch the street and see the window at the same time.

Sara gently pushed open the door. It creaked a little, then swung inward. She held her breath. *Just do it*, she told herself. She took a step forward. And then the door opened the rest of the way.

And a coffin came sliding out.

CHAPTER 19

Sara screamed. She leaped back as the coffin came toward her.

"Hey—get out of the way," a man's voice shouted. "Stupid kids!"

Sara felt Mandy's hand on her arm. "Run!" Mandy yelled. Sara obeyed. But as she looked back over her shoulder, she realized what was happening. The men who worked in the funeral parlor were wheeling a coffin through the door. They were going to load it into the long black car that stood at the curb.

Sara stopped and stood panting on the sidewalk. She watched one of the men lock the door behind him. A wave of despair washed over her. That was it—the end of her last hope.

"Sara!" Mandy called from the corner.

Sara trudged toward her. "Well, forget about sneaking in," she said.

"I'm so glad to hear you say that!" Mandy let

out a long breath. "That whole thing was really a bad idea."

Sara shook her head. "But it was my last idea. What'll I do, Mandy?"

"I don't know," Mandy said. "Look, let's go to rehearsal. We'll think of *something*. Let's just get away from here."

"Okay," Sara agreed. Mandy was right. And, after all, she didn't have any better plan. Maybe they would think of something together.

Sara followed Mandy through the auditorium and into the makeup area. She looked without much interest at the table with a lighted makeup mirror on it. Mr. Demetrios had already set out all the stage makeup and arranged folding chairs around the table. The chairs were covered with neatly folded smocks to keep the actors' costumes clean.

"You take one side of the table and I'll take the other," Mandy said.

Just then Jake Stone came out of the boys' dressing room. He was wearing a green leather jacket covered with chains and studs. He passed Mark Ringle, who was also in costume.

"What's that supposed to be?" Mark asked, laughing at Jake's jacket.

"Who cares?" Jake said. "I'm a dead man, remember? I get eaten in the second act. Who cares what a dead man is wearing?"

Mandy grabbed Sara's arm and squeezed it hard. "Did you hear that?" she asked. "A dead man! That's it!"

Sara looked at her friend as if she were nuts. "What are you talking about?"

Mandy handed Sara a long pair of scissors. "Don't you see?" she said excitedly. "You cut Jake's hair—I mean, the dead man's hair, and you don't have to find a *real* dead body!"

Sara thought about it for a moment. It wasn't so very different from getting animal blood from a piece of liver. Was it?

"Hey, Sara." Molly Granger, a ninth-grader, came in and sat in one of the folding chairs.

"You have to do me first," Molly said. "I'm in the opening scene."

"Okay," Sara said. She picked up some foundation and spread it over Molly's face, still thinking about what Mandy had said.

It's a crazy idea, she thought, *but if it works, I won't have to go near a dead body*.

Mandy was watching her. "What do you think? It's worth a shot, isn't it?"

"It can't hurt," Sara agreed, dusting eye shadow on Molly's lids. She picked up a dark lipstick and pulled off the cap.

"What can't hurt?" Molly asked.

"Um—this lipstick," Sara answered. Her mind was racing. How would she do it? What would she say to Jake? *Think*, she ordered herself.

Out of the corner of her eye she saw Jake walk by again. *The hair from a dead man . . .*

"Heyyyy," Molly yelled. "Stop it!"

Sara looked at Molly and gasped. The lipstick was smeared all over her face!

"Oh, I'm so sorry!" Sara cried. "Um—I think I need some air." She threw down the makeup and picked up the long pair of scissors.

"She's, uh, not feeling so good tonight," Mandy said quickly to Molly.

Sara ran after Jake. He and Mark were going over their lines in a corner.

She hid the scissors behind her back. "Uh— Jake, listen," she began, talking fast. "I—um—I really want your makeup to be right. I mean, you don't want to look weird, right?"

"Yeah," Jake said, eyeing her warily. "So?"

"So the best makeup goes with your hair color. So I thought—if it's okay with you—that I'd cut a little piece of your hair, so I can get your makeup color absolutely right for the performance tomorrow night."

"Cut my hair?" Jake shook his head. "No way, Sara. Sorry."

Sara held out the scissors. "Come on, Jake. Just a little piece," she pleaded.

"Hey!" Jake backed away from her. "Watch it! Are you nuts?"

"Come on, Jake," Sara said again. Her voice rose, getting louder and higher. "You've got to!

Please! Just let me cut one tiny piece—"

She lifted the scissors and stepped forward. Jake backed away from her. "Cut it out!" he cried.

"What's with her?" Sara heard Molly say. "Is she wacko or something?"

Sara turned around. A bunch of kids were staring at her. Suddenly she realized how she must look, backing Jake into a corner, waving a pair of scissors at him.

She dropped the scissors onto the floor and turned around in confusion.

And then she saw it.

CHAPTER 20

There it was—lying on a nearby chair. The wig! Mandy's mother's old wig—made of *human hair*. The hair from a person who was probably dead!

Ignoring everyone's stares, Sara grabbed the wig and ran.

In her room, behind her closed door, Sara pulled the wig out of her backpack. She cut off a lock of hair and sat staring at it. The hair from a dead person.

The door to her room creaked open.

Sara leaped to her feet. "Elizabeth?" she cried in alarm.

Michael's head poked through the door.

"Michael! You're supposed to be at Max's!" Sara couldn't believe he was there.

"I couldn't stay there," Michael said. "I couldn't stop thinking about the third task."

Secretly, Sara was glad he was around.

Elizabeth wouldn't be glad, of course. And Michael couldn't come into the living room with Sara, but it was good to have somebody in the house with her, just in case.

Sara glanced at her clock. "Michael," she said softly. "It's almost midnight. Elizabeth will be here soon." She clutched the lock of hair. "Stay here. Don't come anywhere near the living room. Promise."

"I could just wait outside, in the hall," Michael said. "I'll be completely quiet, I swear."

"Forget it, Michael!" Sara ordered. "This is the *last task*. We can't take any chances. Stay here." Sara took a deep breath. "Wish me luck."

She reached the living room just as the clock began to strike midnight. Moonlight streamed through the tall windows. Sara glanced anxiously at the carvings on the mantelpiece. The moonlight edged closer to the fireplace.

Sara's heart raced in excitement. She held the lock of hair to her chest, took another deep breath, and closed her eyes.

THUMP!

When she opened her eyes, Elizabeth was there.

Elizabeth's cheeks were flushed and her eyes sparkled with excitement. She was glowing, Sara thought, as if—as if she were filled with moonlight.

"Did you get it, Sara?" Elizabeth clasped her hands.

Sara held out the lock of hair. Elizabeth sighed with relief.

"What should I do now?" Sara asked.

"When the moon is ready, burn the hair."

Sara took a matchbook from the mantel. She knelt and laid the hair on the cold marble of the hearth.

What would happen when she burned the hair? she wondered. Would Elizabeth suddenly spring back to life? No, that was impossible. Elizabeth had said she would go to her grave in peace, once the evil was gone. Sara felt a pang of dismay. She would miss the quirky little ghost.

"Are you happy, Elizabeth?" Sara asked.

Elizabeth gave her a quiet smile. "Oh, yes. I've waited so long for this. Thank you, Sara. I owe you more than you'll ever know."

Before Sara could answer, the bright ray of moonlight that shone through the window became even brighter, stronger than Sara had ever seen it. The beam streamed past her shoulder. Sara turned to watch as it moved up the sides of the fireplace.

It struck the carving of the full moon. The carving shone with a blinding white light. The moonlight spread and covered the mantelpiece. The whole fireplace seemed to glow.

"Now," Elizabeth said softly, behind her. "Light it now."

Yes! Sara wanted to cheer. *We've done it!*

She lit a match. The small flame leaped into life. She touched the flame to the hair. There was a sharp, acid smell. Some of the hairs curled up and skittered across the marble hearth.

For a moment there was silence.

Elizabeth's voice called out in a stunned whisper. "No!" she said. Her voice got louder. "What have you done? Are you trying to trick me?"

Sara looked around her in confusion. "Trick you? No, I—why—"

"No!" Elizabeth screamed. "That's not real hair!"

Suddenly, Sara realized her mistake. She had been in such a hurry to get out of the auditorium, so desperate to finish the third task, she hadn't stopped to make sure which wig she was grabbing. She was burning artificial hair.

Beside her, a spark of flame flickered from the ashes of the hair. The flame grew larger and larger.

Sara sprang to her feet to avoid being burned. The flames jumped out, nearly scorching her face. She turned away and glimpsed a sight that made her blood run cold.

My dream. My nightmare. I made it come true!

Elizabeth—sweet, eager Elizabeth—had

turned into a skeleton. The bones gleamed cruelly in the flickering light.

Sara's stomach knotted. She felt sick.

"Elizabeth!" She could barely get the word out. What had she done?

CHAPTER 21

The flames shot higher. Sara threw her arm in front of her face and backed away. When she looked up again, the flames had disappeared. And the skeleton was gone.

Sara ran through the living room and into the entry hall. Michael ran up to her. "What's happening?"

"I burned the wrong hair!" Sara felt near tears. "Michael, I've got to help her!"

"How?" Michael asked.

"I don't know!" Sara looked around, feeling frantic. "What was that?" She stared at the ceiling. Had she heard a thump?

"The playroom, Michael! Elizabeth went to the playroom—I know she did. That room is special to her!"

Without stopping to see whether Michael was following her, Sara raced up the stairs. As she reached the first-floor landing, the entire staircase started buckling, rolling and rippling under her feet. The next instant, the stairs gave way completely. Sara was flying through empty space.

Then the stairs reared up under her. They rose and slapped against her, knocking the wind out of her.

Michael landed beside her. He grabbed her hand, pulling her up. Somehow, they made it to the third floor. Sara ran into the playroom, Michael close on her heels.

The room was empty.

"Elizabeth!" Sara screamed. "Elizabeth—don't go! Wait!"

She ran to the heavy tapestry that hung in front of the secret room—Elizabeth's old room—and pushed it aside.

"What are you doing?" Michael cried.

Sara gasped for breath. "The house knows I didn't complete the third task. We didn't beat the evil, so the house is trying to hurt Elizabeth! I know it! But we can stop it. I know we can!"

Sara glanced around the room. Everything was in place as she remembered it—bed, bureau—and one other thing. "Michael! Look!"

Lying on the bureau was the silver hairbrush with the initials E.C. on it. Golden hairs clung to the bristles.

Sara grabbed the brush. "Elizabeth's hair, Michael! Her very own hair!"

The hairs from a dead person!

"We can burn these hairs," she screamed at Michael. "We can still do it! We can still destroy the evil!"

She yanked the long blond hairs free from the brush. The matchbook was still in her hand. She tried to tear off a match, but it fell through her shaking fingers. She took a deep breath, forcing herself to be calm. She tore off a second match and struck it.

"Sara—look!"

The horrible skeleton stood in the doorway. Sara could hardly bear to look at it. She tried to remember the pretty little girl she was trying to help, the girl who had tried to help her. She held the lit match to the golden hair.

"Elizabeth," Sara cried. "This is the *right* hair. *Your* hair—the hair of a dead person. I can still save you—"

"No! Stop!" the skeleton roared. "Don't burn her hair!"

Sara looked at Michael in confusion. *Her* hair? What did that mean?

"But—I—but Elizabeth—" Sara stuttered.

"Did you think you could fool me? Trick me?" the skeleton screamed in a fury. "Did you think it was so easy to get rid of me?"

"Get rid of you?" The match in Sara's hand scorched her fingertips. She dropped it hastily.

The skeleton let loose a shriek so loud that Sara thought her ears would burst. Sara's mind raced. None of this made sense—unless—unless—

"You aren't really Elizabeth, are you?" she shouted.

"Of course I'm not Elizabeth!" the skeleton screamed. "Did you think Elizabeth's ghost would have such powers?"

The skeleton raised its hands. Flames shot out from its fingertips. The skeleton came closer to Sara and Michael, backing them into a corner.

Michael threw a chair in front of the skeleton. The skeleton kicked it aside without a glance.

"You got away from me before, but you won't get away from me this time! You foolish, silly children. Every task you completed only made me stronger. And now I shall use that power to rid the house of you—forever!"

The skeleton's clawlike hands reached for Sara's face. She threw up her arms to protect herself from the flames.

Elizabeth's hairs were still in her hand. Flames caught onto the hair and shriveled the delicate blond strands.

The skeleton froze and let out an anguished wail. "Elizabeth . . . !" it moaned.

Sara thought fast. The hair was the key. It had to be! She grabbed the hairbrush and raised it up high.

"Look what I found," she called to the ghost.

"More of Elizabeth's hair."

The skeleton shrank back.

"You don't like that, do you?" Sara taunted. "You don't want me to burn it." She nodded at Michael. "Get the matches."

"No!" the ghost cried. "You must never touch Elizabeth's hair!"

Michael lit a match. Sara held the hairbrush close to the flame.

"No!" The skeleton yelled. "Not my darling daughter . . . !"

"Daughter?" Sara repeated in astonishment. "Elizabeth was your daughter?"

The skeleton swiped at Sara with its arms.

"Quick, Michael—another match," Sara yelled. She brought the brush even closer to the flame. "Go away—or I'll burn every bit of your daughter's precious hair!"

The skeleton lunged at Sara, trying to knock the brush out of her hands. The match fell from her fingers and onto the brush. A sharp smell filled the air as the hairs on the brush began to burn.

"Nooo!" The skeleton took a step backward. Was it Sara's imagination, or had it begun to fade?

"Another match, Michael!"

Michael lit a third match. Sara pulled more hair from the brush and held it to the flames.

She watched the skeleton hopefully. Could she make it disappear? *Please, oh, please,* she chanted to herself.

BOOM! The flames shooting from the skeleton's fingers exploded into a solid sheet of bright flame, covering its bones in fire from head to toe.

The flames grew more intense. The air seemed to have been sucked out of the room. Sara gasped for breath, horrified.

Then a ghostly whisper echoed around her. "You've won this time," it said. "But I will be back! Jonah Carter will not be defeated. Never! Never . . ."

An instant later the flames died out. A pile of ashes lay in the place where the skeleton had stood.

Air seemed to rush back into the room, stirring the ashes on the floor. For a moment the ashes glowed with an eerie intensity. Then the glow became hazier and hazier until the ashes had disappeared completely.

"Look! What's that?" Michael pointed to the place where the ashes had been. A pattern had been burned into the wooden floor.

Sara walked toward it cautiously. "J.C.," she read out loud. "J.C.—for Jonah Carter."

Michael whistled softly.

"He's the evil," Sara said. "He's the evil spirit in this house."

The evil was still in Moonlight Mansion.

Waiting to get stronger again—unless they could destroy it.

Sara sighed. "I wonder," she said. "I wonder if knowing who he is will make it any easier."

"Make what easier?" Michael asked.

"The next time," Sara said simply.

CHAPTER 22

The house was quiet. More quiet than usual. As Sara walked down the stairs from the third-floor hallway, they were firm under her feet. The walls stayed where they were supposed to stay. The ceilings didn't drop down and the doors didn't try to slam shut on her fingers.

"It's nice this way," Sara said. "Almost as if it were a regular house."

"Yeah," Michael agreed. He looked tired.

"I really thought—" Sara shook her head in disappointment. "I really thought, this time, we could win. I thought we could really make this a normal house."

"It wasn't your fault," Michael said. "He tricked us."

"I guess," Sara said. "I wish I'd never believed that ghost in the first place."

"You sort of had to believe it," Michael said matter-of-factly. "Because, what if the ghost were telling the truth?"

What if?

"You couldn't know that Jonah Carter was going to trick us," Michael added.

"Trick *me*, you mean." Sara shook her head sadly. "Trick me into *helping* the evil instead of destroying it."

"Well, he didn't win," Michael pointed out. He paused. "I wonder what would have happened if you'd burned the right hair?"

Sara hadn't stopped to think about that yet. "Maybe *we'd* both be ghosts by now," she said. "Real ghosts." She shuddered. "He must really hate us."

Michael punched Sara lightly on the shoulder. "Hey, who cares, Animal Girl? He might be smart—but we were smarter."

They had reached the main hallway. Sara looked around. Everything looked neat and clean, the way her mother liked it. No one would believe that there had ever been a weird ghost in the living room. Or a skeleton that shot out flames and then disappeared—but threatened to come back again soon.

Just then the front door creaked open.

For an instant, Sara's heart leaped into her throat.

"Sara? Michael?" Their father came into the hall.

"Dad!" Sara cried in relief. She threw herself

at him and flung her arms around his waist. Michael did the same.

Mr. Buckner hugged them both in surprise. "What a welcome! But I thought you weren't staying alone in the house tonight?"

Sara and Michael exchanged a look. Alone? They were never alone. The evil was always with them.

"We changed our minds," Michael said.

"Yeah, Dad," Sara added. "I mean, after all—what could possibly happen to us in our own house?"

Don't miss the next

House of Horrors

book

#6 Night of the Gargoyle
by Lloyd Alan

Michael has always hated the stone gargoyle perched atop Moonlight Mansion. When the hideous statue falls from the roof, narrowly missing Michael's head, he knows his instinct was right—the gargoyle is bad news. But Michael has no idea just how bad things are going to get. Because the gargoyle is out to trade places with him . . . by turning him into stone! Can Michael and Sara find a way to stop the evil statue—fast?

And look for these other
House of Horrors adventures

#1 My Brother the Ghost
by Suzanne Weyn

Sara and Michael Buckner have a bad feeling about their new house. It's not just the creaky floorboards, the strange noises, or the flickering lights—somehow Sara and Michael know Moonlight Mansion is haunted!

There's an evil spirit living there and he's trying to take over Michael's body. Sara must think quickly because Michael is fading fast. Can Sara save her brother? Or will the House of Horrors claim another victim?

#2 Rest in Pieces
by Suzanne Weyn

The Buckner dog, Gruff, is the best friend any kid could have. But Gruff has made a horrifying discovery in the backyard—something that's not quite human. And it's turned him into a ferocious beast!

Sara and Michael can't control him anymore. The disembodied claw Gruff's dug up is scary enough, but when the ring it's wearing sttarts glowing, they know something is terribly wrong. Somehow Sara and Michael know it's alive!

#3 Jeepers Creepers
by Suzanne Weyn

When Michael and Sara discover a hidden room
in their house, they wonder why it's been closed
off for so long. Then they notice a strange purple
egg under the bed. What could it possibly be?
All too soon they get their answer: A family of
horrible half-insect, half-rodent creatures hatch.
They're creepy. They're crawly. They're killers!
And they're multiplying fast. Can Sara and
Michael get rid of the creatures before the creatures get rid of them?

#4 Aunt Weird
by Lloyd Alan

Michael and Sara can't explain why they get the
shivers when Aunt Wendy arrives at the door of
the Moonlight Mansion. Their new babysitter is
very strange—so strange that the kids give her
the nickname Aunt Weird. And creepy accidents
happen after she comes to the house. Sara and
Michael start doing things for no reason at all—
as if they'd lost control of their own bodies! But
the real terror begins when Aunt Weird takes
off her head! Will Sara's and Michael's be next?